TAKING CONTROL: RICK'S STORY

MORGAN MALONE

Copyright © 2018, Deborah Sabin

Taking Control: Rick's Story

Books > Fiction > Romance Novels

Keywords: romance, erotic romance, military, Alpha males, second chance

Trade Paperback ISBN: 9781717351449

Print Release: June 2018

Editing and Interior Format by Deelylah Mullin

Cover Design by Kris Norris

ACKNOWLEDGMENTS

Thank you to the many readers of Out of Control: Kat's Story, who requested (some demanded) Rick's Story. I wrote this book for you.

Thank you to my writing group, Writing Womens Minds, for all your constructive criticisms. Maggie May, Posey and Gracie, I rely on you to keep me on track and you always do.

Thank you to my Beta Readers, Sue, Susie and Katie, for finding the mistakes and holding my hand.

Thank you to my friend/mentor/editor, Dee Mullin, who fixes my words, cleans up my typing and walks me through every step of the process. Not one of my books would be in print without Dee.

Thank you to Kris Norris, who with few words and ideas from me, crafts gorgeous covers for my books. I love every one of them.

Thank you to Gayle Tzemach Lemmon's book, Ashley's War: The Untold Story of a Team of Women Soldiers on the Special Ops Battlefield. It is a wonderfully written account of the women who became part of the Army's Cultural Support Team. Their inspirational careers helped me create Britt, who I hope does honor to their lives and service.

Finally, and most importantly, thank you to the Saratoga WarHorse Foundation. The men and women who founded and operate this unique program that matches retired thoroughbred race horses with veterans suffering from invisible wounds of war are the true heroes and heroines of this book. From the day I learned about this remarkable program, located just minutes from my home in Saratoga County, New York, I knew the characters in my book must be linked to this Saratoga WarHorse. I thank them for the time they took to talk to me about Saratoga WarHorse, especially Bob. Any mistakes or misconceptions about Saratoga WarHorse are mine and I apologize for any inaccuracies; I tried to capture the essence of the program and all the good that it does for our veterans of so many wars and conflicts. If only one reader finds help there or can direct a veteran in need to Saratoga WarHorse, I will consider this book to be a major success. A portion of my profits from the sale of this book will be donated to the Saratoga WarHorse Foundation to continue their amazing work.

To my "adopted" son, T, the soldier prince, who served with honor in Iraq and Afghanistan: for all the information and encouragement and for giving me my heroine.

To my fellow members of the Keuka College Class of 1975 Unofficial Reunion Weekend: for brain-storming, feeding me and giving me a quiet, inspired place to finish this book.

And for MLH. Always.

CHAPTER ONE

The tang of the salt air hit Rick before he saw or even heard the Atlantic Ocean. He rolled down the window of his battered green Jeep and took a deep, cleansing breath. A calm he hadn't felt in months began to spread through him—almost, but not quite, reaching his troubled soul. Nine months since he had been down the Shore. Nine months of running away, nine months of searching.

Springsteen was singing about glory days on the radio. Rick sang along for a few bars then abruptly switched off the radio. His glory days were long behind him. *Not that any of my days were glory days.* Hard to glorify any of the campaigns, missions and damn stupid forays the government had sent him on over the last twenty-five years. Mud, dust, dirt and blood comprised most of his memories. The silence in the Jeep was filled by the crashing of waves and the ocean breeze. Cool air flowed through the window, blowing away the heat and humidity of the July evening, washing some of the bitter regret from Rick's face. He glanced in the rearview mirror before he put on his turn signal to leave the highway and cut toward the shore. The man who stared back at him looked weary and old. The highlights in his strawberry blond hair appeared golden in the light but he

1

guessed it was probably just more gray hair. His dark tan seemed to emphasize the wrinkles that creased his forehead and fanned out from the corners of his eyes. Years of facing bright sun and fierce winds were embedded in those lines.

Zipping down Long Beach Boulevard, Rick caught a few glimpses of the water between the houses. The moon hung low in the summer sky, casting a glittering path across the waves and brightening the road ahead of him. With a great sigh of relief, Rick turned down First Street, then pulled the dusty Jeep into the sand-covered drive of a three-story house facing the Atlantic. Built into the dune, the garage faced the street; access to the front of the house was up a flight of wooden stairs. Rick swung his long, jean-clad legs out of the Jeep. With dusty cowboy boots planted in the drifting beach sand, he paused for a moment. *Home.* Reaching into the back seat, he pulled a worn green canvas bag out and slung a leather computer case over his shoulder. Traveling light meant only one trip up the long flight of stairs to the ocean-facing deck. He paused by a loose brick to feel around under it for his spare key. *Hmmm, not precisely where I left it the last time. What's up?*

Easing his gun from the small of his back, he climbed the deck stairs swiftly and silently. Rick left the duffel and briefcase on the edge of the deck, glanced briefly out at the beach before moving quickly to the French doors to his right. He tried the handle, but the door was locked. Shifting the gun to his left hand, he quietly unlocked the door. Nothing in the open-plan living and dining area, or in the kitchen appeared to be out of place. The space was neat and dust-free because he had called ahead so his cleaning service would prepare the cottage for him—including stocking the fridge and pantry. And wine rack, he noted, as he slipped silently through the room and up the stairs to the second floor. A quick search of the two bedrooms and bathrooms on the upper level revealed nothing and no one.

Still puzzled, with the pistol still in his hand, Rick went back down to the main floor. As he stepped into the living room, he saw a small mahogany box on the couch, weighing down a sheet of folded grey paper. He recognized the box. He had sent enough of them to grieving parents and spouses. Purple Heart. *Kat.*

A wave of regret swept through him, tugging at a heart he frequently maintained had lost any ability to feel. But, he had come close almost a year ago and his brush with the beautiful and brilliant redhead had sent him running away from the inevitable pain and disappointment he knew he would cause her.

I guess she took me up on my offer. His last gift to her had been flowers and a note telling her to use the cottage while he was away, advising he probably would not return until the Fourth of July. The Fourth was hours away, but for a moment he was transported back to the autumn when he had almost fallen in love with the gutsy widow of a JAG soldier who had died in Iraq ten years earlier. A lawyer who had been blown apart by an IED—like so many men Rick had known in the past decade. A fate Rick had narrowly escaped on too many occasions. *I've dodged the bullet so many times. My luck must be damn close to running out. Or it should be.*

He stared at the medal receptacle and message for several minutes. Then, sighing and squaring his shoulders, he sat down on the sofa and eased the short letter out from under the gift Kat had left him. His hands were shaking as he unfolded the heavy grey stationery. The unshed tears in his eyes blurred the bold handwriting.

To Rick. For gallant service above and beyond the call of duty, in honor of all your scars—seen and unseen—this medal is yours. You are an officer and a gentleman—and I will never forget you. Kat

Rick opened the box. *Damn it, Kat. You still know how to get to me.* Inside, resting on velvet, as he knew it would be, was a Purple Heart. Awarded to Kat's late husband posthumously, delivered to Kat by some unremembered officer, accepted with tears and a tremulous smile. And a vacant, sad face that said without words, "What good is this? How will I live without him? I don't want a medal, I want my husband back. But I will take this in his honor and I will hate it and the war that did this to us. And you for being the bearer of this final

3

reminder of how much I have lost." Rick knew. He had delivered such medals to grieving widows, sorrow-stricken mothers, and bereft fathers. Until the day, long ago, when he had gone silent, had disappeared into the secret society of warriors who went unmentioned, unnoticed and with nothing but a helmet sitting on a pile of stones to mark their passing.

For the first time in many years, Rick hung his head and wept.

CHAPTER TWO

He awoke with a start. The room was flooded with early morning light. The sun's reflection on the waves cast dancing jewels across the white walls of the main floor. His head ached, and his eyes were swollen and scratchy. Rick rubbed at them with the palms of his hands. *I can't remember the last time I dropped off like that. What the hell time is it?* A glance at his well-worn watch told him it was six o'clock in the morning, Eastern time. He stood and stretched, rotated his stiff neck, bent his sore knees and cursed all the aches in his bones. Too many wounds and too much time in shitty situations had caused scars, adhesions, and badly healed breaks. It took him a little longer each morning to get moving and even longer when he had slept sprawled across a sofa, cramped into an impossible position brought on by sudden sleep and too many regrets. He ambled awkwardly to the bathroom off the main room, feeling some relief after peeing, splashing cold water on his face, and brushing his teeth.

As he passed the sofa, he instinctively bent to smooth out the cushions and straighten the bright woven throw that had slipped to the floor. And the box and letter that had fallen on top of the throw during his restless slumber. Rick carefully placed Kat's token and pledge on a gleaming granite counter in the kitchen before he set up the coffee maker. Once it was gurgling, promising a hot shot of caffeine within minutes, he retrieved the mahogany box and gray stationery and, with a cautious glance around the room, moved quickly to the large seascape on the wall opposite the doors to the deck. Swinging the frame carefully away from the wall on soundless hinges, he uncovered a small wall safe. The door opened silently after he entered the combination, revealing several manila envelopes and a black metal gun box. He checked the box to reassure himself that the Glock and its ammo were still there waiting for him, then closed and locked the weapon away before gently placing Kat's offering on top. *Thank you, darlin'. I'll treasure this more than you could ever know.* The scent of coffee drew him back to the present and he quickly closed the safe and replaced the painting.

He stood before the French doors to the deck, with a large mug of steaming black brew cradled in his hands, letting its warmth take away some of the chill that had surrounded him for the last several months. *I'm freezing. And it's not the air-conditioning. It's my damn frozen heart.* Rick pushed the doors open, letting the heat of the sun and the smell of the ocean sweep into his house. He stepped outside, breathing deep, relaxing just a little. *Yeah. This is what I need. A summer at the Shore, a few projects, and plenty of quiet—then I'll be back to my old self.* Chuckling as he mentally reminded himself of just how "old" his self was, Rick raised the cup to take a long sip of coffee.

He saw the figure emerging from the waves almost directly in front of his cottage at the same moment he heard the loud barking of a nearby dog.

What the hell?

She was a modern-day Botticelli's *Venus*, with the waves foaming around her legs. Long, long legs, lean and tan, disappeared into a bright blue bikini bottom, just visible under the blue and white swim T-shirt that covered a long, muscular torso. Her arms were raised, her hands brushed back sodden strands of platinum blond hair. A swim mask dangled from her left elbow, dropping down into her hand as she lowered her arms. When she stepped from the surf, the woman gave an all-over body shake, drops of ocean water flying off her, glistening for an instant like diamonds in the early morning sun. Then she dropped to her knees so suddenly that Rick lurched forward, splashing coffee as he looked down for a place to leave the heavy mug before he rushed to her aid.

He needn't have bothered. From the deck of the cottage to his left, a huge yellow dog was bounding down the wooden stairs two at a time in a mad dash to the woman. She stretched out her arms to the animal just before the happy hound collided into her, rolling her into the sand. The woman's laugh floated on the ocean breeze. Rick straightened, still grasping his cup of coffee and stepped back into the shadows cast over his deck by the second-floor balcony. From his vantage point, he watched the woman ruffle the dog's fur, the animal prancing and shaking in spasms of pure pleasure. When had he ever experienced such unfettered joy? Rick couldn't remember. A long, long time ago...maybe.

Who was she? The owners of the cottage next door were an older couple who spent half the year in Florida and half the year on the Shore. *Could she be a granddaughter or niece? Or had the couple decided to rent this year?* Rick made a mental note to contact his property manager who handled many of the shore homes and make inquiries. He had not planned on having to deal with a stranger; he just wanted some peace and quiet.

The woman and dog were walking up from the water's edge. Rick eased toward the open doors of his living room, thinking to disappear into the shadows. He just didn't feel like an early morning encounter with anyone, certainly not the mermaid with those incredible legs who was ambling slowly in his general direction. He stopped suddenly when something caught the corner of his eye. A glint of sunlight on metal. He reached for his pistol, but his waistband was empty. *Damn. What is that woman doing with a diving knife strapped to her right bicep? Who the hell is she?*

CHAPTER THREE

Britt's breathing was finally under control after her long early morning swim and rough tussle with a yellow Lab who weighed almost as much as she did. She rose to her feet and started to walk back toward her aunt and uncle's beach house. Alex ambled across the sand beside her, his wet nose touching her hand every few steps as if to reassure his doggy brain she was there, she was okay. She was just that—just okay. She had survived, and she was home. Home in the USA. Grateful she had found a place to live while she put together the pieces of her broken life. *And my broken body.* There was still a slight hitch in her gait and her right leg was throbbing like a bitch. Her shoulder muscles were twitchy and tightening up after her swim. Anticipation of a long, slow soak in the hot tub on the deck of the cottage momentarily distracted her. She briefly closed her eyes and sighed, thinking of just how good the hot swirling water would feel on her aching muscles and healing bones.

As her eyes opened, she caught a flutter of movement ahead of her, on the deck of the cottage next to hers. Imperceptibly, she slowed her approach, scanning the structure. There in the shadows, under the balcony, was a man. Her heartbeat quickened—adrenaline rushed through her system—as she came to full combat alert. *Enemy. Intruder.* Then the voice of reason whispered in her brain. *No, not an intruder.* The house had been opened yesterday and aired out by the cleaning crew while she watched from her deck. Groceries and a case of wine from the shop around the corner had been delivered before the doors were locked and the crew departed. Her eyes focused on the man. The white mug she saw him raise to his lips calmed her even more. *Definitely not an intruder.* He must be the elusive Rick that her aunt and uncle had mentioned when they brought her to the Shore in May. *Damn. I wanted a summer of peace. Maybe he'll leave as quietly as he came. Probably not—my luck has never been that good.*

Shrugging her shoulders to appear nonchalant and also to ease the spasm near her collar bone caused by her sudden tensing at the sight of the man, Britt gradually changed the angle of her path toward her own wooden staircase. She continued to watch the shadowed figure out of the corner of her eye. Her combat knife was strapped to her right arm, protection from sharks—both the ones who swam in the ocean and the ones who skulked on land. She had learned a painful lesson many months ago: never turn your back on a man and never, ever, ever be without a weapon. She had the scars to prove the wisdom of her new mantra.

As though he sensed her unease, Alex pressed a little closer to her side. His head was up, and his tail had stopped its happy wagging. He, too, was on alert and wouldn't leave her.

"Easy, boy. Heel to me. That's my good boy. We're going home. We're just going to get home." She gently patted the damp yellow fur on his head as the two of them made their way to the first of the twelve sandy stairs that led from the beach to the deck. The dog still by her side, Britt stepped up, leading with her left leg. She was supposed to go up each step with her good leg. *Up with the good, down with the bad*, the orthopedic surgeons had instructed her, *ad nauseum*. But, she did not want to reveal any weakness to the stranger who still watched her from the shadows. So, she lifted her right foot to the next step. Healing muscles screamed as she put her weight on the still-stiff knee and pulled herself up by sheer force of will. And a death grip on the stair railing. She hoped her grimace might pass as a smile, but she doubted it. Alex slowed his steps to match hers. She rested her right hand on his sturdy back and took the next step. *Up with the good.* But, up with the bad on the next step, pain shooting down her calf, scar tissue around her reconstructed knee resisting the acute angle. Two more steps to the landing. Britt gained the small platform where the stairs angled ninety degrees to the left. Toward shadowed stranger's house. She bent and gave Alex a fierce hug and a whispered thank-you. Six more to go.

"C'mon, boy. I'll race you!" The dog turned to look at her, as if asking "Are you sure? Are you crazy?"

But as soon as her left foot touched the next step, Alex leaped ahead, taking the stairs at his normal pace of two at a time. By sheer force of will, Britt followed him, hands on both rails, pulling herself up the remaining steps in what she hoped would pass as a gleeful race with her dog. Gasping in pain and satisfaction, she reached the deck. Alex sat waiting by the sliding patio door, tongue lolling and tail wagging a happy beat on the weathered planks. Britt turned toward him. Four more steps and she would be within the sanctuary of the cool interior of the cottage. As she pulled open the glass door, she snuck a peek from the corner of her eye to see if she was still being watched. Just before she stepped inside, mystery man raised his white mug in a silent salute. Their eyes met. The heat from his glance burned straight to her soul.

Britt ducked into the cottage's cool interior and quietly slid the deck doors closed behind her. Her heart beat a tattoo in her chest and she gasped for breath—both from her exertion in racing up those last steps *and* from the stranger next door. *Fuck, fuck, fuck.* She bent at the waist, hands resting on her quivering thighs as she sucked in air. Alex moved in front of her, in silent support. His warm tongue licked against her hand, as if to say *I'm here, I'm with you, everything will be okay.*

"Thank God for you, buddy." Britt caressed his ears with both hands, causing his powerful tail to sweep across the floor in a joyful rhythm. "I don't know what I'd do without you. I'm still such a *fucking* mess!" The dog looked up at her with melting brown eyes as if to reassure her that he wasn't going anywhere.

Straightening, Britt stepped around her loyal dog and headed for the kitchen. Filling his bowl with cold water first, she then reached into the fridge for a bottle of Gatorade and a bag of cheese cubes. Leaning against the counter, she gulped the lemon-lime liquid straight from the bottle while she tossed every other cheese cube into the air for Alex to catch and swallow in one movement. She popped her share of cheddar into her mouth between swallows of the energy drink.

She was way below what she called her "fighting weight" of 150 pounds. Her 5-foot 8-inch frame did not have an ounce of padding on it, except for her boobs. At the end of her recovery and the beginning of her rehab, she'd say, "Hardly any muscle and no butt left, but I've still got the girls." She'd laughed at herself, then as she laughed now.

After taking one last sip from the near-empty bottle, she tossed it in the recycling bin by the door down to the garage.

Looking with longing at the hot tub out on the deck, Britt opted instead for the large walk-in shower in the bathroom that was part of the master suite just off the main room of the cottage. She stripped off her almost dry swim T-shirt and shrugged off the bikini bottoms, awkwardly bending down to retrieve them before dropping them in the bathroom sink for a quick rinse while she waited for the shower water to heat up. Wringing out her swimming gear, she left it on the granite vanity top to hang on the deck later. "C'mon, Alex, I'll rinse that sand and salt off of you in here." By the time she slid the glass door of the shower open, the dog was by her side. She sprayed him with the hand-held shower head after she had washed her hair and soaped off the remnants of her ocean swim. Always an obedient soldier, the dog waited patiently while Britt dried off and wrapped the huge bath sheet around her slender body. She rubbed Alex vigorously with the large towel embroidered with his name. Within a few minutes she was wearing her now regular attire—sweatpants cut just below the knee and an over-size long sleeve T-shirt, pushed up to her elbows. Gathering her swim gear and Alex's towel, Britt stepped out onto the deck to drape the items on the drying rack tucked in the sunny corner near the hot tub. Alex leapt up then flopped down on one of the chaise lounges nearby, letting the sun dry him and lull him into a doggy nap. Britt wanted to join him on the other chaise but decided against it. Her sleep was disrupted enough. If she took a nap, which she longed to do—just drifting away in the warm sunlight—she would be up half the night. And she had work to do.

Back inside, Britt stood at the kitchen counter and went through the exercises for her knee prescribed by the physical therapist. Stretches, lunges, and squats, she moved through the program like an awkward ballerina at the barre. It was nothing like the Cross-Fit routines she had done for years, to build muscle and endurance. After a half hour of gentle movements, she was sweating and breathing hard. It had taken several operations to reconstruct her shattered knee. Months in various hospitals and rehabilitation centers to save her leg and get her back on her feet. But not back to her normal life. *Shit, what's normal? I don't even know anymore. Who am I now? And what is next for me?*

Shaking off her self-doubt, Britt rustled up a high-protein break-fast, scrambling eggs and broiling turkey sausage and tomatoes. Adding whole-wheat toast and green tea, she settled at the bistro table that looked out on the deck and the Atlantic Ocean beyond. She ate methodically, forcing herself to eat everything on her plate, save for a piece of sausage and a bit of egg that would go to Alex.

One year ago, she would have sucked down everything on the plate and asked for seconds, maybe thirds. But, she would still have saved scraps for her faithful dog. One year ago, she was a whole woman. One year ago, she still believed in God, country, and true love. One year ago, she had been Captain Brittany Elizabeth Capshaw, with a brilliant career ahead of her. She was—a year later—a thinner, paler, weaker image of the muscular, tanned, invincible woman who had gone to war.

Stop! A pity party is not gonna make things better and is only going to sap what little strength you have. Britt shook her head, trying to toss the negativity from her mind as easily as she had tossed off the drops of salt water when she emerged from the ocean that morning. *I'm alive. I'm all in one piece.* She flexed her reconstructed knee and shrugged the shoulder crisscrossed with scars. *I'm home. Well, not home—but at least I'm back in the USA, living in a damn comfortable cottage with a kick-ass view and ocean access.* After years in the desert of Iraq and stark landscape of Afghanistan, she still barely believed she could walk out her door and be within steps of the ocean. The Jersey Shore was a far cry from the rivers and lakes of her youth, but she had come to love the sound and smell and feel of the ocean. And it's never-ending power. *And I've got Alex with me. My one true love.* Being reunited with her unit's canine companion upon her return to the States had helped Britt finally begin the recovery process in earnest. Weeks in Germany before she was strong enough to travel to Walter Reed Hospital, then months of surgeries without her friends or comrades-in-arms had been the loneliest time in her life. News that Alex was available for adoption had brought the first genuine smile to her face that her doctors and nurses had ever seen.

A plaintive whine brought Britt out of her reverie. Alex sat at the door, waiting for entry. Grabbing her breakfast plate in one hand, Britt opened the door to let him in. His nose immediately found the plate and his tongue lapped up the breakfast scraps in one long swoop. Britt laughed at his unabashed thievery of the sausage and egg. She ruffled the fur on his head before she grasped the door to close it. All motion on her part stopped when she saw the man next door sauntering across the sand toward the water. A soft sigh escaped her lips as she watched him and wondered.

He was tall and lean, but well-muscled—evident by the taut flex of his thighs and calves as he strode across the soft sand. Tanned, too— all over, by the look of the golden skin stretched across those long legs and the skin peeking out from under the cut-off sweatshirt he wore over loose khaki swim shorts. Strong summer sunlight glinted off strawberry blonde hair laced with gray caught into a stubby pony tail. When he reached the water's edge, he half turned and she saw he had a mustache the same reddish-blonde color and light eyes. And, when he pulled the ratty gray sweatshirt over his head and tossed it on the beach, her breath caught at the sight of six-pack abs and a hard chest lightly dusted with gold and silver hair. *Damn.* He turned back to the ocean, striding purposefully into the crashing waves. And that is when she saw the scars. *Double damn.*

CHAPTER FOUR

E very muscle in his body was screaming, *Old Man, are you out of your mind?* Rick was struggling to cut though the surf and reach the shore. The half-hour swim out and back from his beachfront that, in the past, had barely left him winded was sucking the breath out of his lungs with fingers of fire. His arms felt like lead and his feet were so cold he could no longer feel them. *With my luck a damn shark is going to take a chomp and rip my leg off at the knee and I won't even know it until I try to stand.* He half-laughed derisively at his gallows humor, finally able to relax as his toes brushed the sand. It took a few moments to gain his balance against the strong pull of the tide, but at least he didn't fall on his ass as the waves swept the sand out from under his feet. Finally reaching the towel and sweatshirt he'd left on the sand, he uttered a short prayer of gratitude, cut-off before it left his lips. He didn't believe in prayer. He didn't believe in any power stronger than his own guts and the loyalty of the men he had led. The ice around his heart didn't allow for prayer or hope. Or love.

The sun-warmed towel absorbed the icy water from his skin and the droplets of salty cold from his hair—which hung over his ears and dripped down his neck. He'd lost the rawhide tie that had held his hair when he started his swim. Cursing the frozen rivulets running down his back and chest, he vowed to cut off the long locks that had not been touched by scissors since he'd left on his last mission. Swiping the damp towel across his face, he mentally added a good shave to his list. His bedraggled mustache was long enough to catch in his teeth. "I look like a fucking pirate," he laughed at himself. *Or a mercenary,* which was a damn sight closer to the truth. He wrapped the towel around his waist and, turning toward his cottage, pulled the hot sweatshirt over his head. His head popped through the ratty neckline and his movements slowed. Eyes focused on the still figure that hovered just inside the door of his neighbor's beach house. He casually slipped his arms through the sleeves of the worn grey fleece. His right hand slid down to the zippered pocket on his cargo shorts, lightly tapping the hard object nestled there next to his thigh. Like the elusive blonde who watched him warily from the shadow of her deck, Rick never swam unarmed, even if all he carried was a Swiss Army knife.

Wondering if he was going to be playing cat and mouse with his elusive neighbor for the entire damn summer, Rick sauntered straight up the beach, aiming for the small path that cut between his property and the cottage where the tall, well-armed, skittish woman was staying. He admired the way she stood frozen in position, appearing to barely breathe. That motionless but alert pose convinced him that she had been well-trained in either combat or espionage. *Or both.*

He knew she could not tell whether he was heading for his cottage or hers as he continued his seemingly aimless stroll across the sand. But she didn't move. And her eyes never left his face. He was only ten paces away from the alley between the properties when she finally stepped back from the doorway, turning slightly to grasp the sliding glass door and pull it closed. Before her arm had fully extended, a muscular mass of light yellow fur and flashing white teeth barreled between her legs. The low ominous growl reached Rick's ears just as the Labrador Retriever's feet made their first thud on the weathered boards. Rick stopped dead in his tracks, his only movement was his fingers slowly unfastening the button on the pocket of his cargo shorts. Before he could reach for his knife, the woman's voice rang out in a sharp command.

"Halt. Alex, halt!" The dog careened to a sudden stop at the top of the stairs, but its teeth were still bared, and the growling had not subsided. Moving swiftly, the woman grasped the dog's collar and pulled up. Immediately, the dog's butt hit the deck and the growling ceased. But his gaze was pinned on Rick.

She stood there before him like a Valkyrie. Pale blue eyes roved over him suspiciously, analyzing and cataloging every inch of him. He saw the slight flare of her nostrils when she realized what must be in his pocket. Never looking away, Rick's hand slowly withdrew from his shorts. He spread his fingers to show her there was nothing in his hand. The ocean breeze tossed her long, wavy, silvery-blonde hair around a face that was both arrogant and intelligent. But the faint tremor in her hand as she brushed the hair over her shoulder revealed just how nervous he made her. Her arms were covered by a faded blue, loose-fitting, ratty T-shirt, the V-neck gaping just enough to show some angry red scar tissue running from her collar bone back across her shoulder and disappearing into the shirt. Baggy grey cut-off sweatpants hung precariously from narrow hips, evidence that she was thinner than when she had gotten them. Weight-loss probably caused by the knee injury not entirely concealed by the cut-off sweatpants. He could see the evidence of a long incisions that ran down the center of her knee-cap, a sure giveaway that she had had knee replacement or reconstructive surgery—or both—within the last year. She stood ramrod straight—*Oh, she was military for sure; spooks tended to slouch*, he thought derisively. Leaning slightly to the left, favoring the right leg, leaning a bit into the dog for both support and control.

Rick relaxed just enough to let a slight smile play across his lips. He raised his right hand slowly, past his waist, his chest and shoulder, until his fingers rested against the side of his brow, in an insolent salute. "At ease, soldier," he murmured. "At ease."

That put the remaining steel into her spine. She drew herself up into ramrod stiff military stance and threw a salute right back at him. "That's *Captain*, to you, *Marine*."

19

Her retort wiped the grin off his face. *How did she know I was military, much less that I had served in the Corps?* He dropped the salute and as his arm lowered he saw the tattoo on his inner arm that must have given him away. The tattoo he'd gotten when he finished Basic Training. The Marine Corps insignia. A globe, pierced by an anchor, with an eagle perched on top—Semper Fidelis on a ribbon curling beneath. She had great vision and she knew her military insignia. It made him wonder if she had any ink on that long, lean body. And the thought of finding a tattoo on her shoulder blade or hip bone or at the base of her spine made him harden. *Damn. Put that right out of your mind, Marine.* He sucked in his gut and straightened to military stance and flashed her another salute. "That would be *Major* to you, *Captain*. But since we're both out of uniform, why don't we just make it *Rick?*"

Her eyes narrowed. But he could see the worry lines on her face relax. A little. Her hand still clutched the dog's collar, but she leaned into him again, resting some of her weight on him as if standing at attention for even a moment had sapped most of her strength. Her lips quirked slightly into a half-smile and his gaze was drawn to her generous mouth, with a full lower lip just made for biting.

"Okay, *Rick.* Since we're neighbors for the duration and we're definitely not dressed for active duty, I'll cut you some slack. The name is Britt, and this is Alex." She turned then and headed back across the deck, the Labrador falling into step behind her. Before Rick could say a word, she had disappeared into the shaded interior of the cottage and closed the doors.

"Well, I've just been shut down." Rick chuckled as he continued on his path between the houses. When he reached the front of his cottage, he opened up the back of his Jeep and pulled out a large duffel bag. Lugging it up the steps to the deck, he muttered an ongoing monologue about feisty women and loyal dogs. And the attraction he had for both.

After a long hot shower, preceded by some serious hair cutting and shaving, he emerged into the large and airy master bedroom, draped only in a towel. Ocean breezes cooled the second-floor suite that faced the Atlantic. It was definitely summer at the shore. He could hear the voices of sun worshippers, surfers, and little kids drifting up from the beach. Not nearly as many as would be making a ruckus on the public beach about a mile away but still more people than he preferred to have to deal with while hanging out at his private sanctuary. *God, when did I become such a curmudgeon?*

Standing in front of the full-length mirror, Rick let his gaze wander over his battle-scarred body. White lines crisscrossed his taut, tanned skin. He could identify each battle or skirmish that had marked his flesh. Bullet wound from Somalia. Knife slash from Bosnia. IED blast from Iraq. Burn suffered in Colombia. Stupid scar on his left index finger from trying to cut limes when he was too drunk to see in Las Vegas. Turning slightly, the small cluster of bullet wounds high on his back came into view. A souvenir of Afghanistan. The first visit.

"For a highly paid, much in-demand military consultant and former Marine, I tend to get shot, cut, and blown-up way too often. I'm stunned anyone wants to hire me for anything more complicated than taking out the garbage." Rick snickered at his dark humor. He had to put it all in perspective. He was still alive. He'd served his country's interests. It was his fifty-first birthday and damned if he didn't look not bad for 51—especially after his impromptu haircut and shave. And there was a beautiful blonde next door with a story to be told.

But how to overcome the cautious female's reserve? He was nothing if not a master strategist—that's really why the government kept calling him into sticky situations. A shudder passed through him as he pulled on a subtle Tommy Bahama print shirt over khaki shorts. His casual beach attire was out of synch with sudden memories of cold desert nights when men died, and women wept. Shaking off the dark memories of his checkered past, he headed down the pale wooden stairs to the main floor. It was time to breach the Captain's defenses.

CHAPTER FIVE

Britt had changed into a long caftan-like robe. July nights even at the Shore were warm and humid. The thin cotton was cooler than sweats and a long-sleeved shirt, covered up all her scars, and its brightly colored swirling folds made her feel like a woman. Why she wanted to explore her femininity was an elusive and slightly offensive unknown to her. For so many years, she had sublimated every feminine instinct into pure drive and focus on her missions. In a profession that valued above all else macho, physically superior, and supremely confident men, she and the women she had served with had initially modeled themselves after the men they interacted with every day. It was not enough to excel—the competition had to receive a total ass-kicking. If their male counterparts could run 25 miles in full gear, the woman aspired to run 25 miles in full gear, faster than the men. Given the obvious differences between men and women, there were some areas that the women could not beat them—but it didn't stop them from trying.

Britt laughed at her image in the mirror. It had been a long time since she had dolled herself up, as she referred to the few minutes she had taken to twist her long hair up into a messy knot, darken her blonde eyelashes with some mascara, and spritz on a little citrusy scent. She'd even slipped some turquoise studs into her pierced ears, smiling at how they made her eyes appear an even deeper blue.

"Hell, it's the Fourth of July. I should dress up to celebrate America's birthday. Maybe I'll even break out a bottle of bubbly." She glanced over at the rug where Alex watched her with doggy amusement, his large head resting on folded front paws. "C'mon, boy, let's make a fancy dinner."

The dog leapt up at the sound of his favorite word and pranced ahead of her out the bedroom door, tail wagging. Alex made a beeline to the refrigerator. Soon, he was in doggie heaven as Britt began pulling chicken and cheese out of the fridge, followed by everything necessary for a huge summer salad. She'd grilled the chicken and some corn the day before using the mammoth gas grill out on the deck. And, glancing out her kitchen window in the direction of Rick's cottage, she was thankful for her foresight. He was lounging on one of the chaises, a long-neck bottle of beer hanging from his fingers, fragrant smoke wafting from the domed grill nearby. With his well-muscled, tan legs stretched out, his head leaning back against the cushions, he was the picture of sexy beach relaxation.

Ignoring the sudden dryness in her throat and the slight tremor in her hands, Britt busied herself with cutting up chicken and carrots for Alex and mixed in some dry dog food for crunch. As her dog chewed up his dinner in record time, she turned to the mass of veggies spread out on the kitchen island. In short order, she assembled a combination of greens, avocados, tomatoes, peppers, and cucumbers—to which she added chunks of chicken, queso, and corn. With quiet efficiency, she blended together the ingredients for a spicy Ranch dressing. A nice Tex-Mex salad was going to hit the spot. She actually felt some hunger pangs as she reached into the cupboard to pull out a bag of corn chips to go along with the salad. "Now, all I need is some Corona and this celebration can start."

Standing in front of the open refrigerator door moments later, she had to concede defeat. There was no Corona on ice in the fridge, though she didn't remember drinking the last one. While there was a twelve-pack in the pantry, it was not cold, and she didn't feel like waiting. "Damn, I can either forget the beer or drive to a convenience store on the Fourth of July—which is *not* happening—or drink something else." She was not drinking anything too strong. She had gone without alcohol of any kind during her recovery. And then she had drunk too much upon her release from the hospital. And she just didn't feel like wine. "Oh, just get over it, girl, and open up a can of seltzer." But, she slammed the fridge door anyway just to show how pissed she was. The sound was music to her ears.

The rapping on the door to the deck made her jump and turn quickly around. The Marine was standing there, grinning like a fool, a six pack of Corona in one hand and a plate of steaming barbequed shrimp in the other. *What the hell!*

Alex was immediately by her side, butt down, nose near her hand, quivering in anticipation of her command. Rick snapped to attention but ruined his military stance by shooting her an ingratiating grin. A thousand warnings flashed through Britt's brain and she almost turned away and headed to her bedroom. But the thought of another evening alone made her pause. The need to spend Independence Day with someone who knew first-hand the cost of the freedoms the holiday celebrated, had her murmuring to Alex, "Stay, boy. It's okay. Stay."

Rick's grin widened into a genuine smile when she moved across the room and unlocked the latch on the patio doors. As Britt slid them open, she was greeted by the balmy evening breeze and the sound of celebrations up and down the beach. "Can I help you? I didn't order a takeout delivery tonight." A giggle almost escaped her lips at the confused expression on Rick's face. *Did he think I was just going to open the door wide and welcome him in? He's got balls.* The sudden flash of annoyance almost had her shut the door in his face.

"Hi. I know this is rather presumptuous of me but it's my birthday today and its America's birthday and I just didn't want to celebrate by myself. But, if you have other plans or would just rather be alone, I can just leave this shrimp for you. I made too much. But I'm taking the beer back; I'll need all of it to drown my sorrows." His last words were a bit smart-ass, but they did not mask the sincerity of his request. And she saw the same need for camaraderie in his eyes that she often felt herself.

"Far be it from me to sentence a Marine to a solitary birthday celebration. Why don't you put the shrimp and beer on the table over by the grill? I'll get some plates and cutlery." Britt stepped back into the kitchen where Alex still sat, whining and thumping his tail. "Are you okay with dogs? He wants to say hello." She called out to Rick as she reached for the salad.

"I love dogs." his voice echoed from the deck. "Especially Labs."

"Go, say hello, Alex. It's okay." The dog leaped through the door, butt wiggling and tongue lolling, the picture of doggie hospitality. His eagerness to greet Rick sent a small shiver of regret through her. Alex missed being around people, around men. They had been living a solitary life for the last few months since they'd been reunited. Alex was used to dozens of people being around, mostly guys, during the time he'd spent with her unit in Afghanistan.

Hoisting the huge salad bowl in one arm and plates, knives, forks, and napkins in the other, Brit made her way out to the deck.

Rick was down on one knee, rubbing her wiggling dog's belly and crooning nonsense to him in a deep, teasing voice. "Oh, you're just a big baby, aren't you? You don't scare me now that I know your weakness. You're a belly rub junkie, aren't you? Aren't you, you big handsome boy?" He looked up as Britt approached, then stood, taking the heavy salad bowl out of her right arm.

She jerked at the almost electric shock of his fingers brushing along her inner arm.

He must have noticed her reaction because his eyes widened then narrowed as if considering what to do about it.

She stepped away from him and over to the teak wood table set under a jaunty umbrella. Laying out the place settings, she said "It got so hot this afternoon, I thought I'd have to eat inside, but the breeze seems to be sweeping the heat and humidity out to sea. It feels good." Her hand reached up to brush the blowing strands of hair from her face. A hand that was trembling from his touch.

"Do you want glasses for the beer? Or is out of the bottle okay?"

He was pulling bottles covered with drops of condensation from the six-pack.

"Bottle is fine for me. Here," she said as she reached for the remaining beers, "let me take those inside and put them in the fridge so they stay nice and cold. I've got some lime slices cut up. I'll get them." Rick held the carton out to her and she made an effort not to move her fingers away from his. Once again, she felt sparks all along her nerves at the touch of his fingertips on her hands. She could feel heat rise to her cheeks, so she turned quickly away.

"The salad looks amazing!" Rick called to her through the open patio doors. "I think it will be great with the shrimp. I'll just go ahead and open the bottles."

Britt re-emerged with a small bowl of lime wedges in her hands. Placing it on the table, she grabbed a lime wedge, rubbed it around the neck of the Corona and let it plop into the pale golden brew. Raising the bottle, she tilted it toward Rick in a silent toast, then took a long sip.

"God, I love Corona. I was just standing in front of my fridge cursing myself for not putting any on ice when you knocked on the door. I had resigned myself to a can of seltzer." She took another swig of beer. "So, I owe you one for that, Marine."

He grinned and took a swig of beer himself. "Hmmm, I look forward to collecting that debt, Britt." He put the bottle on the table, wiped his hand on his shorts and held it out to her. "Let me introduce myself properly. I'm Rick Sheridan. I own the cottage next door and have for a lot of years. I was in the Marines for a lot of years, too. I've been out for a while now and I pretty much make my living as a consultant on films and books about the military."

She would not have pegged him as a movie consultant. He still moved with military precision. And something else. A wariness, an alertness, and a sense of leashed energy emanated from him. Britt would have thought he was into espionage. Or war. Just like her. She swallowed her bitterness and reached out to take the offered hand. "I'm Britt Capshaw. This cottage belongs to my aunt and uncle and they lent it to me for the summer. I'm in...I was in...the Army. Now, I'm not. Let's eat."

They passed the next couple of hours in pleasant small talk, enjoying the good food, cold beer, and refreshing ocean breezes. Alex nosed around both of them, snapping up any crumb that fell, and tidbit that was offered until finally he was satisfied and stretched out on one of the sun-warmed cushioned chaise lounges.

Britt was reluctant to talk about her career in the Army, something she would have chattered about nonstop just a year before. Her scars were too raw; both the physical and emotional damage still too painful to discuss. She was pleasantly surprised Rick did not pry into the details of her military service. Neither did he share much about his time in the Marines.

The sun was starting to sink behind the cottage, and the sky was deepening from robin's egg blue to indigo. Light wind coming in from the ocean cooled them and was starting to wreak havoc with the remnants of their meal. Rick rose and began piling plates, napkins, and silverware. "I'll bring these in and grab us each a cold one, if you'd like."

Reaching for his empty bottle, Britt nodded her agreement. "I'll toss these in the recycling bin. Just leave the dishes in the sink, I'll get to them later." She felt relaxed for the first time in almost forever and a small, contented smile played across her lips. Alex raised his head at her movement and gave a mighty canine stretch. He was just getting to his feet when she heard the first blast.

She froze. Beer bottles tumbled to the deck, the sound of glass shattering only adding to her terror. "Incoming. I say again, incoming." The words were a whispered scream. Britt's eyes were blank, staring with horror at a scene only she could see. Alex jumped off the chaise and was immediately at her side. Her hand fell to the top of his head. "Go, boy. Go. Get the children out. Move those women against the wall. Soldier, get those children out of here." She pushed against him. He ran to the edge of the deck, his whimpers and yips echoing across the distance between them. Then he ran back to the open patio door.

CHAPTER SIX

Rick had just gone into the cottage when he heard the sound of firecrackers erupting from the street in front of the house. "Damn early for the fireworks display from the public beach just up the shore from us. Must be kids setting them off," he thought, just before he heard the beer bottles crashing on the deck. Plopping the dishes in the kitchen sink, he turned and dashed through the open doors. Britt stood frozen in place, all color drained from her face, her eyes staring blankly out to sea. Alex was running back and forth between her and the stairs, frantic to find...something.

"What's going on?" Rick rushed to Britt's side. Then he heard her, heard words he had said himself in the thick of an attack. "Incoming. I say again, incoming. We're surrounded. I've got civilians. I've got women and children. I say again, civilians. We need to evacuate. Where are you? Where are you?"

Instinct kicked in. Rick moved in close to her side. "Message received, Captain. Move your civilians out. Choppers standing by. Enemy is contained." His voice was one of command and she responded like the good soldier she must have been.

"Message received. Moving out. Rendezvous in...where's Nadia? Where is Nadia?" Britt started to crumple, almost falling into his arms, as she came back to the present, to reality. He grabbed her by both arms, pulling her into him, steadying her. Alex was at his feet, whimpering, looking from Rick to Britt and back, as if waiting to be told what to do next. As Rick lowered Britt into a deck chair, he spoke to the anxious dog. "Okay. It's okay, Alex. Stand down."

Brit slumped in the chair, her head hanging down, hands loosely clasped on her lap. Her breathing was shallow and labored. Grabbing a bottle of water from the table, Rick lifted her chin, intent on getting some liquids into her, even if he had to pour it down her throat. But when he tilted her head back, he saw the tears coursing down her cheeks, utter anguish in her eyes. "Oh, darlin', it's alright. It's okay now. Just take a drink here and you'll feel much better. Here now, just take a little water." He tilted the bottle up to her lips and she took a small sip, her throat working as if it were too painful to swallow. Rick used one of the extra napkins to wipe the tears from her face.

She jerked at his touch, turning her face away from him. Her slouch disappeared, as she straightened in the chair, her posture erect. "What are you doing?" she snapped, pushing at his hands. "Don't touch me."

Rick sat back on his heels, taking in her transformation from help-less female to snarling woman warrior. But he knew who, or what, he was looking at: another vet and another flashback to yet another battle. He'd suffered such flashbacks himself, so he knew the fear and loathing she was feeling at the moment. And he knew what she needed.

"You had a flashback. Probably brought on by the sound of fire-crackers. I hate those damn things. Sound like an M16 at close range."

Her eyes opened wide, color stained her cheeks. "What are you saying? I did what?"

"I heard some firecrackers out front, then I heard beer bottles dropping on the deck. When I found you, you were standing here, issuing orders about evacuating civilians. Alex was in a state, running back and forth between you and the stairs." She was staring at him, disbelief giving way to dismay.

Rick got to his feet. "Look, just sit here for a minute and get your bearings. I'll get you something to drink then I want to clean up this broken glass. Will you be okay here with Alex?"

Britt started to protest but her dog interrupted her, pushing his head up under her hand, demanding that she focus on him. Alex rested his paw on her knee, as if to comfort her and to anchor her in place. She looked up at Rick and nodded.

He made quick work of finding a broom and dustpan, picking up the larger pieces of the shattered beer bottles and sweeping the remaining glass shards through the open deck planks. He also found a bottle of Jameson Irish Whiskey and two short glasses in a cupboard in the kitchen island. Plopping the bottle and glasses on the table, he gave Alex a chunk of chicken he fished out of the salad remnants. The dog gratefully accepted his reward and laid down, his head resting on Britt's bare feet.

"I don't drink whiskey." Her voice sounded rusty, but firm. "I take some meds...."

"You can have one shot tonight. You need it more than the meds." He filled the glass half-full and put it in her still unsteady hand. "Listen to the doctor. I've taken those meds myself and I've drunk plenty of this stuff. This is better for you right now."

A shadow of a smile played across her mouth and almost reached her eyes. Britt raised her glass in a silent toast to Rick, then downed a good portion of the whiskey. Coughing, she reached for the water bottle as if to wash the burn from her throat. Rick knocked back the whole shot in his glass and poured another.

His eyes on Britt, he sat in the chair adjacent to her. "You want to talk about it?"

"No." Her sigh tore at his heart. "But I'm going to have to, aren't I? I've been through this routine before, though not for some time. It must have been the sound of the...firecrackers, you say? I haven't heard them since I've been home. Haven't heard anything that sounds like over there. Like Kandahar." She took another sip of whiskey. "I don't remember what I said."

"Incoming. Women and children. Move them out. Evacuation."

"Oh, well, that could have been any one of several forays. Not an

31

unusual situation for us. We took some fire almost every time we went out." She took another sip of whiskey, her hand steadier this time when she put the glass back on the table.

"You were on active duty in Afghanistan? When?" Rick's mind was working. He'd been in Afghanistan. Recently.

"For a few tours." Britt took another sip of water, obviously avoiding giving him any details.

"You were in Kandahar. Lots of action around there."

"Yeah. We were based there but we were out in the country a lot, too." Her eyes were not meeting his. *What was she hiding?*

"I spent some time in Afghanistan last year. Consulting."

"Really?" Britt finally looked at him, some of her wariness disappearing. "With whom?"

With a bitter chuckle, Rick told her he had been meeting with the Army about the pros and cons associated with the use of non-military security forces. "As my position was not what some of the higher-ups wanted to hear, my time in Afghanistan was cut short. I took some other assignments on my way home, so I didn't get back in the States until recently."

"What did you tell them?" Her voice was almost a whisper.

"I told them soldiers fight wars. Period." He leaned into her space, but she didn't flinch. "I expect you know that as well as I do. Who were you attached to? Rangers?"

The shuttered look returned to her eyes. Britt looked away, swallowed hard, then swung her gaze back to Rick. "Yeah, we were with the Rangers. I was part of the CST. Cultural Support Teams pilot project. I stayed in afterwards and did two more tours in Afghanistan."

"I've heard of that team. Outstanding work."

She smiled at his words.

"So, why did you leave the Army?"

Her face closed up again at his direct question. She looked down at Alex, still curled by her feet. "I don't really want to discuss it with you, Marine. It was personal." Her eyes, when her gaze returned to his face, was cool and distant.

"Well, I know you were injured." At his statement, her hand flew down to cup her knee. "And not too long ago because your scars are still pretty new. So, I'm thinking you were hurt pretty bad and the operations and the rehab took a while and left you not in the shape you need to be in to continue with your duties. You took a medical discharge, even though you didn't want to."

"You don't know me—you don't know anything about me and the Army. I think we're done for tonight. I think we're done." She started to rise.

He was not going to let her walk away; he needed to know what had brought this warrior woman down.

"You mentioned Nadia. You were looking for Nadia." His gaze didn't leave her face.

Tears filled her eyes again as a great sob tore through her, almost stealing her breath. Her arms wrapped around her middle and she rocked back and forth, just crying.

Rick put out a hand to steady her but paused before his fingers brushed her arm. She reached out to clasp his hand, squeezing it with both her hands, holding on like she was drowning, and he was her lifeline.

"We lost her. We lost her that night. I lost her. She was mine and I couldn't protect her, I couldn't save her. I killed her. I killed her."

CHAPTER SEVEN

Britt lay in her bed, one hand stroking Alex, who was stretched out beside her. The dog snuffled softly in his sleep, his paws twitching slightly as he dreamed. The moon hung low over the ocean, casting a silver river of light across the beach. Dawn was fast approaching, and she hadn't yet slept. The waves crashing on the shore were the only sound she heard. Well, that and her uneven breaths.

The whiskey and the meds had done little to calm her, to stop the constant rewind of the tape in her head, replaying her last night in Afghanistan over and over.

She'd told him. There on the deck, her hands locked in a death grip on Rick's hand, her eyes focusing on a distant land and a not-so-distant disaster, she told him. Not everything. She would never tell anyone everything about the attack that had taken her career and the life of her best friend. But, with the flash of fireworks lighting the sky, with booms like cannon blasts echoing in her ears, Britt shared some of her truths and many of her lies with the somber-faced Marine.

Her words came back to her, in the pre-dawn light, and they gave her no peace. She doubted she would ever feel peace again.

Fresh out of graduate school with master's degree in Social Work and a runner's body, Britt had enlisted in the Army—like so many Americans—in the days following September 11, 2001. An Ohio farm girl, she had completed two years of study at Columbia University and just had gotten her license when the jets crashed into the World Trade Center. And the Pentagon. And a lonely field in Pennsylvania.

After Basic Training, Britt had undergone additional training at Officer Candidate School at Fort Benning and had been commissioned as a second lieutenant. Her first deployment was to Iraq, as was her second. She became a first lieutenant and was working as a counselor in the Army's Medical Services Corp, when she learned in 2010 about the creation of the Cultural Support Team pilot program. She was one of the oldest candidates accepted and after months of rigorous training, was shipped to Afghanistan and attached to a unit of Army Rangers. Her mission was to assist her team during special operations in accessing women and children and they information they possessed. The trial program lasted for a year and she was rotated back to the States. After two years training other female recruits, with the repeal of the military's ground combat exclusion policy which kept women out of combat positions, Britt found herself back in Afghanistan. Though not technically an Army Ranger, she was reattached to her former unit based in Kandahar.

She saw active duty frequently, accompanying the Rangers as they helicoptered into remote regions seeking out Taliban strongholds. Her job was to locate any women and children in the compounds they infiltrated and glean from them any relevant information about weapons, attack plans, or the location of wanted war lords. It was demanding, dirty, dangerous work. And she loved it.

Rick's eyes had lit with what seemed to be understanding and appreciation for her dedication and enthusiasm. "I know what you mean. There is nothing as satisfying as being part of a team of trusted comrades, all with the same purpose in mind: defeat our enemies and bring about peace." His words had thrown her for a moment. "Trusted comrades" caused bile to rise in her throat. But, as she had done countless times before, she swallowed her bitterness and continued her story.

One damn cold night in February 2017, she and her interpreter, Nadia, had headed out on a mission with their team. Two helicopters took them about an hour away from Kandahar to a village that was known to be the home of one of their most elusive Taliban operatives. They landed a short distance from the village and managed to enter the compound without setting off any alarms or IEDs. Britt and Nadia had circled around the interior, looking for the separate entrance that usually denoted the women's quarters. Heat sensors had marked several targets they believed to be women and children.

They burst through the door to a cacophony of screams and tears. Four women, six children, and two babies were crammed into a 10- by 10-foot room with no windows and just one door. Nadia immediately moved to calm the women, assuring them that they would come to no harm while Britt called in their location and the number of people they were detaining. Her team leader advised that they had not located their primary target and ordered Britt and Nadia to interrogate the women to ascertain if they knew the location of the war lord.

Moving among the women, handing out treats to the children, Britt and Nadia had begun talking to them about their home, their husbands, and the surrounding area. One woman seemed eager to talk but was obviously being silenced by a glare from one of the other, older, women. Britt was attempting to separate her from the group when she heard a scuffle outside the room. She had just called in their need for assistance to their unit leader, when gun fire broke out on the other side of the door. Relaying the situation to her team, she received no response. With a nod to Nadia, they stepped toward the women, hoping to get them into the corner of the room farthest away from the door, sheltered with the children.

"But, before we could make them understand what we wanted, the older woman began screaming in Pashto. Nadia made a move to quiet her; it was obvious the woman was warning whoever was outside the door that there were two soldiers in the room with them. Amidst a flurry of shots, the door flew open. I saw two armed men starting in, one was getting ready to toss what I think was a grenade. I got a shot off, but the thing dropped from his hand and I watched it start to roll into the room. I grabbed Nadia to put her behind me, but she side-stepped me. I started to fall and must have hit the stone floor with my right knee. I was reaching for her when the device exploded. I fell behind her. She took the full blast."

Britt's eyes were full of unshed tears. She broke her grip on Rick's hand to brush them away. She stared out at the ocean for several moments, composing herself. Remembering. "Nadia was dead. She died instantly, trying to shield me. One of the Afghan women died, too. I think it was the one who was trying to speak to me. And several of the children were injured." She took another deep breath and reached out again for Rick's hand.

"Of course, they didn't tell me about Nadia until much later. I didn't regain consciousness until I was back at the combat hospital in Kandahar. I got some shrapnel in my shoulder. I had a concussion and some bruising from being thrown against the stone wall by the blast. And my knee was shattered. The docs patched me together as best as they could and then shipped me out to Landstuhl. My knee was going to need way more work than they could manage in Afghanistan. I was out of it for most of the flight."

Rick pulled her hands to his lips. "I know, darlin', I know. Been there, done that. Got the T-shirt. And the scars."

"And the medal?" Britt sniffled then whispered the question.

The Marine had straightened where he sat and shook his head. "No, darlin'. Where I've been, they don't give out medals. Not for what I've done. The only reward is living to fight another day." Rick reached out and grasped her chin with his strong, callused fingers, tilting her head up so her eyes met his. "You didn't kill her. Nadia was where she was supposed to be, where she wanted to be, doing her job. You deserved every medal you received and probably a few more. Let the guilt go. Soldiers get killed in wars. It's the simplest and the hardest truth I know."

He'd kissed her forehead then ambled across the deck and down the stairs to the darkened beach. A few moments later, he was at the door of his own cottage. He flipped on the light by the door, then paused in the pale golden arc. Looking back at Britt's deck, where she

38

still sat, hands clasped in her lap, Rick straightened and threw her a salute with military precision. Then he disappeared into the darkness of his home.

Several hours later, as sunlight made its way across the floor of her bedroom, Britt rubbed her fingers across her forehead, touching the invisible brand Rick's kiss had left. Turning into Alex's warm back, she rested her chin on his head and drifted into a dreamless sleep.

CHAPTER EIGHT

He'd slept like the dead. Like the innocent dead. Groaning, Rick rolled over to face the music and the bright sunlight peeking through the blinds on his bedroom French doors. He'd forgotten to close them after he'd stumbled up the stairs to his master suite. He smirked at the thought. He was not feeling masterful this morning. After leaving Britt alone on her deck, he'd hunkered down in his kitchen, sitting on a stool and staring out at the waves through the open deck door, while he made his way through most of a bottle of whiskey. It was damn fine whiskey and he felt more than a little guilty just mindlessly knocking back several shots, but not guilty enough to stop. Not until he'd drowned his own memories of people who had died on his watch, under his command, because of his fuck-ups.

"Oh, good God, Marine, get your skinny ass out of bed and make something of the day. You're 51, you're not over the hill. Yet." As if to prove to himself the truth of his words, he rolled out of bed and onto the floor. Fifty push-ups later, he had sweat the alcohol out of his system and loosened up his muscles. He pulled on gym shorts and a faded gray T-shirt and headed downstairs to grab a cup of coffee that he could already smell brewing. Thank God, he thought, that he'd been just sober enough to program the coffeemaker the night before. Coffee first, then a run on the beach, before the holiday crowd closed in. Once he was in the kitchen, mug of caffeine cradled in his hands, he let himself remember the vulnerable and courageous woman he had kissed and left the night before.

"What was I thinking?" A gulp of steaming coffee almost scalded his throat. "I wasn't thinking, at least not with my main brain." He ruefully glanced down at the bulge in his shorts, brought on by simply remembering a chaste, comradely kiss. "Down, boy! She's not ready for you, yet." *And, I don't know if I'm ready for her.*

An hour later, he was sweaty, limber, and his mind was not on Britt. At least not so occupied with her that he had not been able to run. Stumbling back up the stairs from the beach to his deck, he was surprised when he saw her shades were still down and there was no sign of movement in her tidy cottage. "Not my problem," he reminded himself as he showered and dressed for another hot day at the Shore. After a second quick cup of coffee, and a glance out at the empty beach, he opted for action rather than sitting around all day waiting for Britt or Alex to appear.

Rick rarely used the interior staircase to the lower level, but he wanted to avoid the sight of Britt's empty deck. Down the wooden stairs he went, through a small storage room and into his equally small garage. He hit the garage door opener as soon as he entered the cool, dark home of one of his greatest treasures: his antique MG convertible. He hadn't driven it since he was last on the Shore and it was time. Yanking off the dust cover, he admired its shiny navy-blue finish and the pale gray leather of its interior. Over twenty years since he found it in Miami, bought it for a song, and drove it up the coast. That trip had also found him this cottage, his other beloved possession, when he pulled off the Garden State Parkway to get a glance at the Atlantic Ocean and to look up an old friend.

Easing himself behind the steering wheel, the soft leather seat cooling his skin, Rick sat for a moment, just appreciating how lucky he was to be home, to have a home and a car and another year of life. Too many friends lost—to drugs, alcohol, PTSD. Too many dead and forgotten by the nation they had fought and died for—and sadly, too many who had forgotten their comrades-in-arms. "Not today, Nellie, not today." He ran his hand over the smooth leather dash of the car he had named for his grandmother, then started it up. The engine leapt to life with a low growl of power and within minutes he was out on the street, zipping down Long Beach Boulevard to Beach Haven.

If anyone could put a grin on his face and put his demons to rest, it was Mick Mullarney. Pulling into Beach Haven Foreign Cars Sales and Service, Rick felt most of the tension leave his neck and shoulders. Before he was halfway across the parking lot, the double glass doors to the showroom swung open and a giant of an Irishman burst into the sunlight. "Well, boyo, I figured you'd be finding your way down here sometime today. But this is a bit early for drinking, even for you. That means you've got worries. What is it this time? Our beloved Uncle Sam or a woman?" There was a lilt of the Irish in the voice of his friend, even though Mick had been born and raised in the New Jersey suburbs of New York City. But his parents were Irish immigrants as was the Irish grandmother who had lived with his family until she was well into her eighties. When he was drunk, or angry, or moved by emotion, Ireland crept into Mick's voice.

He swallowed Rick in a great bear hug that almost lifted him off his feet. "Turn yourself around, my man. If you're here to talk, and I can see that you are, I'm going to need something to drink and a bit of food. Head on down the road to Nardi's and we'll drown your sorrows in eggs and bacon." Mick released Rick and, before he had time to do anything more than nod, his friend had climbed into the passenger's seat of the low-slung car and was tapping his fingers on the dash as if to telegraph his wishes to be off.

"The car is running great, Mick. Thanks for looking after her while I was gone." Rick glanced over at his friend as he pulled out of the lot.

"Don't mention it, boyo. My pleasure for sure to run this sweet thing up and down the Boulevard every week or so. The ladies do love the sight of a handsome Irishman in a beauty of a car. They start chasing *me*." After Rick shot Mick a baleful stare, his friend roared with laughter. "I get you every time! Do you really think I'm picking up women in your beloved convertible? First off, there aren't that many women around from October to at least April. And the ones that are here are pretty much spoken for. And I'd never do that to your car." Mick laughed again, then sobered. "And I wouldn't do that to Annie."

"I know, Mick. But, it's been five years, my friend, that Annie's been gone. You know she'd kick your ass, if she was here, for putting her up on a pedestal and worshipping her from afar. She'd want you to get on with your life. I know it and you know it, too."

"And how has this conversation turned back around onto me and my dead wife, God rest her soul, when I'm the one who was laughing and joking a few minutes ago and you were the one who arrived before I was barely opened looking like the dog that had been kicked by its master. And then made to sleep outside." A grin was playing across Rick's face as his friend continued. "All night. In the rain."

Rick was finally laughing, unable to contain his amusement.

"You're right. You know me too well." Rick swung the car into a spot in front of the restaurant. Within a few minutes, they were seated inside the cool interior, steak and eggs ordered and Bloody Marys on the way.

"Before I begin the serious questioning, how is that little grandson of yours? Did you get to spend any time with Ricardo?"

"He's great! I'm a lucky bastard that my son let me stay in his life and has included me in his family. The little guy is amazing! He's three and he knows all his numbers and letters, in both English and Spanish! He calls me Abuelo Rick!" Laughing, Rick handed his cell phone to Mick, the background set to a photo of a black-haired, brown-eyed little boy playing on the beach.

"You are a lucky SOB, my friend. Is this from October or did you get back there once your *assignment* was completed?" Mick gave the phone back as their Bloody Marys were delivered by their waiter. He raised his in a toast, "What doesn't kill us, makes us stronger."

They both laughed out the last word of their private toast, "Bullshit!"

The spicy cold bite of vodka and tomato juice and the warm camaraderie he felt for Mick, eased the last of the tension from Rick's face. He leaned forward and began to speak in low tones.

"I saw the family last week. On my way home. They are amazing, and the little guy is just perfect." Rick took another gulp of his drink. "But, I took the long way home to get to them. It was bad this time, my friend. Fucked-up-and-everyone-to-blame bad."

"Christ, I figured it would be when you told me where you thought you were headed. Asia is still a shit-hole of major proportions but nothing you haven't dealt with before. But, man, when they *requested* you head west from there, I knew it was going to suck. I said a rosary every day for you and I'm not ashamed to admit it." Draining his Bloody Mary, Mick signaled the waiter for another drink. "Was it Afghanistan?"

Rick nodded. His fingers traced random outlines through the condensation on his empty glass. "Yeah, same shit. Same place." He shook his head in disgust. "Too many good kids over there with too much shit to deal with and not enough support. The private security companies keep getting in the way. Christ, it's a cluster fuck. The Russians were right about one thing, though: you can't win a land war in Afghanistan. You fucking can't do it." He stopped talking when the waiter approached with their breakfasts and two more icy drinks.

For a few moments, the two men dug into platters of meat and fried eggs, hash browns and hot buttered toast, like they hadn't eaten in days. "Man, you don't get food like this in California." Rick laughed and pushed his plate away. "My son and his wife are into breakfast burritos, which I love, and avocado toast, which I'm okay with, but it's just not a real breakfast. You know what I mean?"

Wiping his last piece of toast through the runny yolk of his egg and popping it into his mouth, Mick nodded. "I hear you. My daughters keep making me fruit smoothies and granola bars. They bring them to me at work. I don't mind the fruit shakes, but I've got a drawer full of those damn granola bars."

"We've eaten worse."

"Yeah, there were times we would have killed for granola bars." They stared past each other, their eyes blank and their minds focused on distant memories.

"So, Afghanistan was bad? You were out of Kandahar?" Mick was drinking coffee now, his attention directed at his former comrade-in-arms.

"Yeah, it was rough, but I knew it would be. What followed was worse. The worst I've ever seen. I don't know if I can do that again." Slumped in his chair, he looked and felt ancient. "It wasn't Afghanistan, Mick, that did me in."

"Where? Can you tell me?" His friend almost whispered the request.

"Head west from there. Past Iran."

"The Kingdom?"

"No, but close." Rick's eyes met his friend's eyes. Realization dawned on Mick's face.

"Fuck, you were *there*? Were you exposed to any of that shit?" Mick grabbed Rick's wrist as if to reassure himself that his friend was okay.

"No, I was there two months ago. They said just to go and look around. I did, and in some places, it looked like progress was being made but there was something just not right. You know what I mean. And the damned Russians were all over. Everyone was tiptoeing around them. It's a damn fucking mess." Rick took the last sip of his Blood Mary and almost slammed the glass down. "And then I left, and the shit truly hit the fan."

"Damn it. You're right. This has got to be it for you. You're too old for this shit and I'm too old to be sitting here on the fucking Jersey shore worrying about you running around in fucking Syria." The last words were a whispered hiss from Mick.

Rick just shook his head, agreeing with his friend. They had both seen too much of man's inhumanity to man in the years they served together in the Corps. Mick had been a graduate of Clarkson with a degree in Engineering when they met in Special Ops training. They were posted to the same dangerous mission fresh out of training— two still-wet-behind-the-ears first lieutenants without a clue. Rick was on reconnaissance and Mick was with his squad manning the tanks that supported the Marine's efforts in Somalia. They returned a year later to their brides and new babies as battle-scarred, bruised and battered veterans of too many skirmishes and too many deaths.

They were back in Africa too soon, back in battles that no one at home heard about and they could not talk about—even to each other. When they returned to the States, Rick's wife wanted a divorce, Mick's wife wanted another baby. Both women got their wish. The two men rose through the ranks and frequently served together in remote locations across the world. Rick became more adept at the black ops aspect of the military while Mick mastered all the machinery the Corps could throw into a battle.

Until 2006. In Iraq. They were part of US Naval and Marine forces working with Iraqi military to push through to Ramadi General Hospital, which was being used to treat Al-Qaeda injured, torture Iraqi police forces, and fire on US troops. At the very end of the effort, while troops were searching for IEDs hidden around the hospital, Rick was interrogating captured insurgents. Armored Marine vehicles under Mick's command were taking position around the perimeter when a lone sniper emptied five shots into Mick before US forces killed the shooter. He almost died twice on the flight to Germany, his lungs filling with blood. He survived with part of his right lung removed and the loss of his right middle finger.

When Rick finally hooked up with him at Ramstein, Mick was coughing and cursing the damn insurgents for costing him the ability to tell them to go fuck themselves. Rick was relieved to find his best friend still alive and still feisty. But his relief was dashed when Mick told him he was taking a medical discharge.

"Man, I can't sit behind a desk. You know it would drive me crazy. And they won't clear me for active duty—no way—with a missing lung and fuck-you finger."

Rick couldn't argue with him, but *he* couldn't leave.

Mick headed home to his wife, Annie, and two daughters. They'd saved enough for him to build a foreign car sales and service center on Long Beach Island, near Mick's home on his beloved Jersey Shore. Five years later, Rick left the Marines, too, after twenty years of service. And came "home" to Jersey and Mick's family.

Unfortunately, over the next several years, Rick kept getting called back into "situations" that needed his expertise. It made putting down roots almost impossible. Mick looked out for his property in New Jersey and Rick's cousins kept an eye on his apartment in his "hometown" in Upstate New York. He traveled to and through the West Coast which allowed him to spend some time with his son, daughter-in-law, and grandson. But no time for romance. And no inclination to "settle down with a good woman", which Mick's wife, Annie, was always nudging him to do.

Sadly, Annie lost her battle with breast cancer while Rick was away on one of his *consulting* trips. He'd made it back to Jersey just hours after she breathed her last breath. At least he had been able to support Mick through the nightmare of burying a vibrant 45-year-old woman. And a piece of his heart. Fortunately, Mick's two daughters lived close by the old man and both came to work at the car dealership. To temporarily help out, they said—and they did. But mostly, they kept an eye on Mick. The girls made sure he was dressed in clean clothes, ate at least a decent lunch, and showed up at work. Mick often remarked he owed his life to them. "I swear, those girls just henpecked me so much that I just got too pissed off to be depressed."

The two old friends, old soldiers, sat staring at each other, seeing the images of lost battles and dead men in each other's eyes. Rick was the first to break the silence. "Yeah, I think I'm going to hang around the Shore this summer. I might head up to Cambridge for a week in August when the Track in Saratoga is open, check out my place above the store, but I need to be near some water, some really huge amount of water, after months in the desert."

"Well, the Atlantic is certainly big enough and wet enough for you, boyo. And it doesn't hurt to have *Wonder Woman* living next door, either." Mick just grinned when Rick gave him the finger. "Yeah, I've met Miss Britt a few times. She was as skittish as a new colt when I first saw her a month or so ago when I went over to take Nellie for a spin and get the storm shutters off your French doors. She and that almost white devil dog of hers just stared at me from the shadow of her deck overhang. Never said word and never took her eyes off me. She was still using a cane then."

"She's not using one now. I saw her coming out of the ocean yesterday morning like Botticelli's *Venus*. With a nasty knife strapped to her arm. She spotted me on the deck when she was about halfway to her cottage. I swear she ran up the steps of her deck just to show me that she was in top physical shape, but I could see the scar on her knee. That stunt cost her. I bet that knee was throbbing like a bitch all day."

Mick took another sip of his now cold coffee and grimaced. "Do you think it's too early in the day for a beer?" Mick laughed and signaled the waiter to come over.

"Like the song says, man, it's five o'clock somewhere." He ordered two Coronas and waited until the waiter had moved off to fill the order.

"She's military, but I guess you figured that out."

Rick nodded in agreement and waited until the waiter was back with their beers and had gone again. "I saluted her from the deck. She bolted. And she called me on it later. Tried to pull rank on me. Can you believe that shit?" He took a sip of beer, let the cold brew trickle down his throat.

Mick was laughing. "You didn't tell her you were a Colonel, did you? That's not fighting fair, boyo, as you only held that rank for what…like…fifteen minutes?"

"No, almost two weeks, you lowly Captain, you." Rick joined in the laughter. Both of them had chafed against the rules more than a few times while serving, losing promotions for conduct unbecoming, then winning rank back with their cunning and courage. "She told me to call her Captain, so I mentioned that she could call me Major." Mick almost spit beer when he heard that.

"You're talking to a beautiful, courageous, fragile woman warrior and your method for getting to know her better is to get into a pissing contest about rank?" Mick shook his head. "Man, if that is how male-female relations are going these days, it's a good thing I'm not interested because I am way out of touch."

"If you ever decide to try it, you'll be fighting women off. With that Irish accent, those broad shoulders, and all the hot cars at your disposal—all you need is a cute dog." Rick grinned at the notion of his friend walking a poodle or chihuahua down the streets of Surf City. "The blonde next door sure has a cute dog. Not cute, really. Handsome. Big, loyal, good-looking yellow Lab. Man, I love Labs."

"You interested in her or her dog? I think she brought him back from overseas. They arrived together in the beginning of May. The guy down at the market told me as how her Aunt Carole had ordered in a load of groceries for her and I know the cleaning crew was in there, too. Said they were told to get the place ship-shape before she arrived then to just let her be. Seems to me she must have had a rough time over there."

"We had dinner last night on her deck. I just invited myself over. We talked a little. She was with the Rangers out of Kandahar and saw plenty of action. I think it's been almost a year since she got wounded. Must have been bad."

Mick looked down at his right hand, flexed his fingers then laid his hand on his chest. "Yeah. It probably was. You know how long it took me to come around and I had you pushing me and Annie comforting me every step of the way. I can't imagine trying to come back from those kinds of battle injuries all by yourself." He finished his beer. "She tell you what happened?"

"Yeah, but I don't..." Mick cut Rick off.

"I don't need to hear the details. I just wanted to know if she can talk about it. That's one of the hardest things to do. If she's talking about it, that's good."

Rick nodded and gulped the last of his beer. They threw some money on the table and made their way out into the sun and ocean breeze. Even though they kept up a conversation all the way back to

Mick's place, Rick's mind was elsewhere. He was wondering what Britt and Alex were doing. If they'd slept in or had gone out really early; if they would be out on the deck when he got home. And he was wondering if Britt would ever tell him the whole truth about what happened to her in Afghanistan.

CHAPTER NINE

A cold wet nose pressed against her cheek. And hot breath blew across her throat. Britt woke to the certainty that it was not the mysterious and sexy Marine from next door who was trying to rouse her. No, it was a hungry and full-bladdered dog who was urging her to get her lazy butt out of bed.

"Okay, okay, okay, Alex." Pulling herself up from the prone position, her knee throbbing and her shoulder stiff, Britt limped out of the bedroom, across the living area to the still curtained patio doors. Pulling the room-darkening drapes aside, she unlatched the door for her wiggling and whining canine companion. Her reward was a paw crushing her foot as Alex dashed across the deck and onto the beach. She had trained him to go under the deck to do his business; it made it easier to clean up after him when she had to let him out by himself. Within moments, Alex was back at the door, yelping to be let inside. He circled her and circled her as she made her way into the kitchen to fix his breakfast. Sharing a piece of cheese with him to give herself a moment to pour a cup of coffee, she took one long sip of the dark brew and sighed. It was an addiction she did not think she would ever kick. Hot coffee in the morning, dark and bitter, was her fix.

After making up a bowl of chicken, sweet potatoes and dry dog food for the ravenous Lab, Britt leaned against the kitchen counter and enjoyed her coffee. And the sight of what was once a skinny, dirty, skittish dog, sucking down food, tail wagging. "We've come a long way, boy." Alex looked up at her with adoring eyes, just for a second, then returned to his breakfast. Britt helped herself to a banana before meandering out to the deck and plopping down on the chaise. Sitting in the shade of the roof overhang, she scanned the beach for any sign of Rick. He wasn't on his deck, but she could see sandy footprints scattered on the steps. "Must have been out early for a swim or a run," she muttered to the dog as Alex came out to sit next to her, his head propped on her lap, eyeing the banana in her hand. She broke a piece off for him.

Even though it was late morning, there were a few people out on the beach; it was another glorious July day on the Shore. It was not too hot yet and yesterday's humidity had been blown out to sea.

"What do you want to do today, boy?" Her hand rested on his silky yellow head. His tail started thumping as he looked away toward the beach.

"Feel like a swim?" At the sound of one of his favorite words, Alex dashed over to the stairs then back to Britt.

"Okay, let me change while I finish my coffee." Britt rose awkwardly, wincing at the tightness in her knee, and tossed the last bit of banana to Alex. It only took her a few minutes to brush her teeth, braid her hair, and pull on a sleek black tank suit and a brightly flowered rash guard. Her aunt had treated her to several swim suits, swim T-shirts, and cover-ups when she had first arrived at the Shore. She had seen the pity in her aunt's eyes at the sight of her scars and emaciated frame; pity made bearable only by the love that was also there and her aunt's no-nonsense attitude.

The sand was hot on her bare feet, so she moved quickly over the beach, Alex at her heels. The both ran headlong into the surf, relishing the feel of the cool water on already overheated skin. Britt played with Alex, splashing the big dog, and chasing him through the waves. At her signal, he turned and trotted back across the beach to lay in the shade of their cottage while she swam.

Her heart was not in a long-distance swim today. Rehashing with Rick even some of the events from her time in Afghanistan had sucked her energy and left her emotionally and physically drained. Britt powered through the water for thirty minutes, praying physical exertion would drive the ghosts from her memory and the ache from her heart. She did not achieve the hoped-for result, so she headed back to shore—her knee looser but aching and her shoulder still stiff.

Britt didn't realize how physically drained she was until she stumbled coming out of the surf. An outgoing wave sucked the sand from under her foot and she started to tumble. But a strong hand grabbed her by the elbow and pulled her back to her feet. Snarling, she started to pull away, but the hand tightened its grip. Before she could push against the hard chest of the man at her side, another wave slapped against the back of her thighs and shoved her against him. It was Rick. She knew it without even looking up at his face. That chest with the sprinkling of reddish blonde and silver hair peeking out of the V-neck of his T-shirt. His strong arms, covered with a light dusting of the same curly hair. The Marine Corps insignia tattoo, faded a bit from age.

"You can snarl all you want, Captain, but I'm not letting go until I get you out of this surf. The waves are coming in hard. There's a yellow flag up—didn't you see it?"

Before she could retort, and she knew she was about to say something bad-ass, they were both hit at the knees and tumbled into the shallow water and strong pull of the ebbing tide. Sputtering and spitting salt water, Britt was the first up, pushing loose strands of hair out of her eyes. Then, she collapsed back into the water, wracked with laughter. Alex was standing next to Rick's fallen figure, his paw on the man's chest, as water lapped over Rick's body.

"Alex, no. It's okay, boy. It's okay. Rick is a friend. Let him up." The Lab just looked at Britt as if he didn't understand the command. As if he was thinking, "This man puts his hands on you and I'm supposed to let him live?" She bent down and tugged on his collar. "Stand down, soldier. That's an order." Alex backed away from Rick and planted himself next to Britt, separating her from the man who was scrambling to his feet.

She couldn't be angry at her dog, he was trying to save her from what appeared to be a threatening male. Not like he hadn't done that for her before, she thought fleetingly. And she couldn't be pissed at the Marine. He'd come up on her too quiet, the sound of the surf drowning out any noise he made and anything he might have been trying to say to her. So, Britt cursed herself for being too distracted to notice him approaching her as she was wading to shore. And she had not worn her knife today—the first time since she's arrived on the Shore—figuring that with all the people about, she was relatively safe.

And she realized she *was* safe. Her gut told her that Rick was no threat to her, no physical threat, anyway. She would have to be careful what she said around him because he obviously knew how to get people to talk. But she knew, absolutely, he would never hurt her body. What he might do to her heart was an open question.

"You want to take a step closer to me, ma'am." She heard the command in Rick's voice. "Let your dog know you are safe with me, that I pose no threat to you. I want to get us out of these waves and I don't think he's going to let me give you a hand."

Britt looked down to see the sand was eroding under their feet at a rapid pace and the pull of the ocean, even in only a few inches of water, was going to unbalance her again as soon as she took a step. She reached out her hand to Rick, speaking to Alex as she did so. "It's okay, boy, Rick is a friend. It's okay." Keeping a watchful eye on Britt, the dog moved away to a spot out of the path of the incoming waves.

At Rick's touch, a jolt shot through Britt's hand and arm like she'd been struck by lightning. Rick tightened his hold on her hand and pulled her toward him. She stumbled and was gathered in his arms. Arms that held her like iron chains, like airy strands. Firm but gentle, sure but tender.

It had been a long, long time since she had been in a man's arms. Even longer since she had felt safe in a man's embrace. Her breath caught, and she stared up into Rick's face to see if he felt her reaction. His eyes were the same stormy blue as the ocean. His nostrils flared, as if he was breathing in her scent. Britt leaned into him, just a slight movement, but it brought the hard tips of her breasts into contact with his damp t-shirt and solid chest. Now it was Rick's turn to suck in a breath, his chest expanding, pushing against her nipples.

She stood in his arms for what seemed like an eternity, her eyes searching his face. Her arms were hanging at her sides. Then she brought them up, so her hands could clasp his arms—she thought—to steady herself. But as soon as her hands wrapped around his biceps, she knew her intent was to hold onto him, to keep him close.

The cool water was barely lapping at her toes, the sun was beating down on her back. Somewhere in the distance she heard the roar of the ocean, the laughter of children and the raucous call of the gulls. But all she was aware of was the beating of her heart. Britt stepped further into him, a slight movement, they were already so close. She tilted her head up, her lips parting slightly and her eyes drifting shut. But not before she saw the desire flare in his eyes, not before she saw his head bend toward hers. Then his lips touched her, and she forgot to breathe.

CHAPTER TEN

H e fought the urge to pull her hands from his arms, to pin them behind her back, while he ravaged her mouth. Pent-up desire and his need to control warred with his knowledge that such an action would likely end with him on his ass in the sand and her dog's teeth at his throat. And her dashing back to her cottage for her knife and safety.

So, Rick kissed Britt like he'd kissed his wife on their first date. Soft and sweet, barely brushing her full lips. His arms around her, steadying her, holding her close but not pinning her to him. It went against every instinct he had followed for the last twenty years. Control was his mantra, it gave him the ability to keep himself and anyone in his care safe and protected. And to guard his heart—so badly damaged by years of war, loss, and betrayal. He was shaking with his need to bury his hands in her hair and nip at her neck.

She sighed and swayed closer, moving into his embrace, her arms reaching around his waist. Her head tilted back farther as she sought to keep their mouths touching—barely touching. He groaned and slid his tongue across her lips, desperate to taste her. Britt gasped and broke their embrace. Her eyes were wide and questioning, as if searching his face for some clue as to what would be his next move. A small yelp escaped her lips when his arms slid down to her waist and under her bottom to lift her and cradle her against his broad chest. Rick took the remaining few steps out of the surf and onto the damp, hard-packed sand. Alex was immediately on his feet, blocking his progress.

"Tell your dog to let us pass, Britt. Let me carry you a little farther. Let me get you back to your cottage." His voice was a harsh whisper.

"I don't need you to carry me, I'm perfectly capable of walking across the beach. You need to put me down, Marine." Her voice was a shaky protest.

"Let me, I need to carry you. Let me." Britt stared at him, her mouth a small O of surprise. She shook her head as if confused by his words. But still she complied with his request. "Alex, c'mon buddy, it's okay. Come with us."

The big yellow Lab fell into step next to them, his nose nudging Rick's thigh as if to remind him he was not alone, that he was under the dog's capable scrutiny. The trio made their way to Britt's cottage where Rick released her from his arms, letting all her long lean flesh slide down the length of his body until her feet rested on the hot sand. His hands were still on her hips, his erection pressed into her belly.

Rick kissed her on the forehead, letting his lips linger on her damp skin, breathing in the essence of Britt. He did not want to let her go but knew he was seconds away from pulling her up the stairs to her deck and into the shadowed interior of her house where he would...what? He wanted her more than he had wanted any woman for years, and he was pretty sure she was attracted to him. But, he was uncertain of his next move. A feeling that had him totally dumbfounded. He lifted his head and let his gaze sweep across her face.

"Baby, you'd better go inside and shower off all that sand and salt that we've been rolling in. Then, climb into your bed and take a nice nap with Alex. You've got shadows under your eyes that are as blue as the ocean. You're beat, and you need some rest."

She got a stubborn look on her face, like she had intended to do just as he ordered but she was pissed he was telling her what to do.

Before she could open her mouth to protest, he drowned her words with a blistering kiss. Then he stepped away.

"Get inside, Captain, before my mouth takes a tour of your body right where you stand. I've got about one minute of control left, then all bets are off. Go inside, now. Please."

Britt stared at Rick for a moment longer, then she stepped around him and moved awkwardly up the stairs, her dog at her side. She paused when she reached the deck, turning to gaze back down at him.

"You may have won this skirmish, Marine, but the battle has just begun. Next maneuver is mine." And she disappeared through the double doors.

It didn't take Rick long to stomp across the sand between their houses and up the stairs to his deck. Once inside his cottage, he threw his sunglasses on the kitchen island. He took the stairs to his master suite two at a time, cursing with every step. His T-shirt was yanked over his head and tossed aside as he moved into his bedroom and his shorts and briefs were off and on the floor of his bathroom seconds later. He stood naked in the huge walk-in shower and turned the shower on full blast, ice cold. "God damn fucking son of a bitch. Mother fucking bastard ass cock sucker." His fist slammed against the tiled wall as freezing water pelted his overheated body but had little effect on his rock-hard cock.

He braced himself with two hands against the wall and let the water run over him, shivering not from the chill but from his need for Britt. He looked down at his still huge erection and sighed mightily. "What the hell. What the fucking hell am I going to do about you, you stupid randy dick?"

Rick closed his eyes, willing his breathing to even out, his mind to regain control over his body. His penis was having nothing to do with what Rick wanted. He could see Britt in his mind's eye, long and lean, tan and blonde, emerging from the surf today just as she had done the morning before, like a mermaid who had become human and was taking her first steps—confident but unsteady. He could feel her thin but muscled arm under his hand as he steadied her, smell the sun and sea in her hair, taste the salt on her lips. The memory of her slight weight in his arms made him groan with need. Surrendering to a desire he could not vanquish, his right hand gripped his rigid penis. Visions of Britt and the practiced movement of his hand quickly brought him to a loud but unsatisfying climax. Disgusted with his lack of control, he turned the water up to warm and soaped himself from top to bottom, cleansing himself of sea, sand, and the passion he'd just released.

Rick threw on a pair of gray gym shorts, went down to grab a beer from the fridge in the kitchen, and plodded back up the stairs to stretch out on the cushioned chaise on the deck outside his bedroom. It was angled away from Britt's house, so he knew she couldn't see him from her deck. The sun was behind his house now. He relaxed on the still-warm cushions, a slight breeze keeping the heat away, the icy Corona trickling down his throat doing little to cool some very hot ideas about Britt he struggled to ignore.

He lay there for several minutes, trying to blank his mind by breathing deeply, focusing on the horizon, the deep blue ocean undulating with the currents, and the waves crashing on the shore. "Yeah," he snorted, as he took another long pull of beer, "this is not working. This is not going to work." Putting the beer bottle down on the deck, he slammed his hand against his forehead in frustration. "Think, you dumb fuck. Think. What the hell are you going to do about her?" He'd never met a woman like her before. He closed his eyes and focused on the past, hoping to find an answer.

His marriage to Elizabeth had been a traditional "fall in love in college, first great love affair" kind of relationship. They had common backgrounds and common goals, both highly intelligent, hard-working, honest, healthy people. Great sex life but nothing too adventurous. They wanted kids, a nice house, money saved for college, secure retirement—the American dream. Then, he had the bright idea of enlisting in the Marines out of college to pay off his student loans. He'd been sent to Annapolis after basic training for advanced courses in language and military intelligence. Elizabeth was thrilled as she found a dream job at the National Institute of Health, which allowed her to work and take courses towards a Master's degree. For two years, life was perfect. They had their son right before he shipped out for Somalia. When he came home, he had to get to know the year-old boy all over again. They might have been able to make the marriage work, but he was shipped out soon thereafter. After another long tour in a battleground most Americans knew little about, he returned to a son who did not recognize him and a wife who didn't want him.

That was the last emotional relationship he'd had. There had been women over the ensuing twenty years—he was no monk, for sure. But, there had been no love and no tenderness. He wouldn't let his guard down and risk the heartbreak he'd known when Elizabeth and his son left him. Rick built walls of protection around his heart and he built a steel wall of control around his passion. If he controlled every aspect of his coming together with a woman, if he was in charge he could protect himself from tenderness and running the risk that a woman would mistake his lovemaking for the real thing. Pain with pleasure became his mantra. That way, sex was never like what he had shared with Elizabeth—that memory was protected. And no woman would mistake his steely command, his domination in bed, for love. He'd opted for brief affairs, except for his disastrous six-week marriage to Sybill, a State Department attaché, with whom he had shared a penchant for poker, vodka, espionage, and some light bondage in Bosnia. The highlight of their relationship was a quick wedding in an Elvis chapel off the Strip in Vegas followed by a quickie divorce in Tijuana when they sobered up.

Until Kat. The prior year, his brief interlude with a beautiful and brilliant Military widow had caused fissures in the walls around his heart. Fearing he could not give her what she deserved, that she would fall in love with him and he would not be able to reciprocate, he'd bolted to the West Coast and then taken another mission to another godforsaken shit-hole of a battle zone. Just to avoid seeing heartbreak in her eyes. "It was the right thing to do," he muttered to himself as he took the last sip of beer. "You know it was the right thing to do. She's better off without you." He knew she was engaged to be married to an old law school friend; he'd seen the announcement in the Albany papers. And he wished her well. No regrets.

No resolution of his present dilemma coming to him, Rick rose and went downstairs to get another beer and fix a sandwich. He ate at the island in the kitchen, deck doors open to let in the ocean breeze and the sound of the surf. He surveyed his living space. His home was beautiful, calming, and simple. Mostly white, with some colorful accents. And not one photograph. Souvenirs from various locations around the world he'd visited or worked decorated walls and table tops, but there was nothing that could not have been picked up by any tourist in any village marketplace. Nothing personal and nothing that could identify who he was, where he'd been, or who he loved.

There was a gnawing emptiness inside him the hoagie and the Corona had not filled. He stretched out on the long white sofa in his living room and closed his eyes. Images of his grandson, Ricardo, and his son John, and daughter-in-law, Inez, played like a family video in his head. He felt great love for them, real affection and respect for the life his son had made. Regret was the only emotion Elizabeth's face brought to mind, and a vague memory of almost childlike happiness.

If he looked back farther, he had some sweet childhood memories of his grandmother, Nellie, who had raised him from the age of four. He'd lived with her in an apartment above her antiques store in Cambridge, New York. He had loved her and the small-town security their life together gave him. His Aunt Susan, her husband, Theodore, and their two daughters, Maggie and Colleen, had been all the family he'd ever needed.

So, he thought as he analyzed his past, he had the capacity to love. But he was not sure he had the strength any longer to do so.

Love! Where had that come from? Britt's face as she struggled from the ocean, her eyes when she told them about her last battle, the scars that did not mar but only enhanced her beauty came to his mind. He'd only known of this woman's existence for about 36 hours and was spinning love stories in his head, reevaluating his entire past, and reimagining love-making as he knew it...with Britt. *Give her time. Take it slow. Let her think she holds the reins. Can I do it?* "Shit. I'm fucked," Rick muttered out loud. "I am well and truly fucked."

CHAPTER ELEVEN

Britt dusted the flour from her hands and sighed with satisfaction. She popped a stray chocolate chip into her mouth before she placed the mixing bowl and wooden spoon into the sink. Looking around the kitchen, she laughed at the mess she had made. But she didn't care. She hadn't baked in a longer than she could remember. The aroma of chocolate chip cookies filled the room, reminding her of happier days in the kitchen of her family home in Ohio. She did a little dance to "Born to Run" playing on her iPad, almost tripping over Alex. The dog had been circling her waiting for something, anything, to drop off the counter and into his mouth. He'd already rescued three stray almonds from the floor and was obviously hoping for more.

The oven's timer interrupted her dance. She removed two trays of fragrant cookies from the oven and placed them on trivets on the island to cool. "Alex, I love this kitchen. It's bigger than most places I've lived in the last ten years!" The dog merely yipped in response, his eyes glued on the forty-eight cookies just inches away from his nose. Feeling sorry for him, Britt reached into his treat jar for a chicken meatball and tossed it into his open mouth. She didn't even make him sit.

"I haven't felt this good in a long time, boy. I guess we really needed that nap." She had followed Rick's direction and curled up for a nap with Alex after they had showered off the salt and sand. She hadn't been able to scrub away the feel of Rick's mouth on hers. Not that she had tried that hard. Her fingers had strayed to her swollen lips, trying to recapture the glide of his tongue. "Get your head out of the sheets, soldier." She'd scolded herself. The scent and feel of him had remained with her and had prompted several very sexy dreams. When she woke up, she was filled with nervous energy. Her knee was too stiff to contemplate an afternoon run and it was too hot, anyway. Tossing aside the nightshirt she'd worn while napping, she pulled a dark blue haltered sundress over her head. It was loose and cool, and she didn't have to put on a bra. Just a pair of the bikini undies she favored. Twisting her hair up in a loose bun, she had padded barefoot into the main room of the cottage. Shadows were casting a cooling shade across the deck and she could see a strong breeze was whipping up whitecaps in the dark blue ocean.

Wandering into the kitchen for a bottle of water, inspiration had hit her. Rick's birthday had been the day before. They had not had a cake or anything to celebrate. It seemed the neighborly thing to do to make him a batch of her favorite almond chocolate chip cookies. She sniffed at the thought of bringing him cookies. She would make very clear that they were a belated birthday offering and not a thank you for rescuing her from the rough surf. "Huh! Like I needed rescuing. Right, Alex?" The dog had wagged his tail, willing to agree to anything if it earned him an almond or a chocolate chip.

The cookies had cooled enough for her to break off a piece and sample their chewy goodness. "Mmmm. Just like I remembered. Not too sweet." At his imploring look, Britt broke off another small piece and tossed it into the air for Alex to catch. He gulped it mid-air. "You didn't even chew it. How can you taste it, you greedy pig-dog." Laughing, she ruffled the fur on his head and bent to plant a kiss on his long nose. "I love you, anyway. Now, go lie down so I can clean up these dishes." Satisfied, he trotted over to the deck doors and curled up on the rug.

Water was running in the sink and her hands were covered with soapy water. She was singing along to "Dancing in the Dark" when she heard Alex's sharp yip. Looking up, she saw Rick standing on the deck, about to knock on the doors. They stared at each other, his icy blue eyes fixed on her, a grim smile on his face. Britt called out to Alex, "It's okay, boy, it's okay. It's just Rick." The reassurance was unnecessary as her dog's tail was sweeping back and forth in an arc across the polished wood floor. Her hands still in the water, she nodded at Rick and he slid the door open. Alex wiggled up to him, looking for a butt rub. Rick stroked the big dog several times, his eyes never leaving Britt's.

Staring at him, she was frozen in place. His long legs were encased in faded blue denim and he was barefoot. A black T-shirt hung loose at his waist but was stretched tight across his muscular chest. The fading sun glinted off his hair, turning it to silver and gold. A braided silver ring flashed on his right hand, a beat -up silver bangle on his opposite wrist. Britt did not think she had ever scrutinized a man so carefully. At least not a civilian. She laughed to herself.

"What's so funny, Captain?" Rick's voice was soft and low as he straightened up from petting Alex.

"I was thinking that Alex and I have both relaxed a great deal, maybe too much, since we got to the Shore. He is putty in your hands. And I'm standing here admiring your jewelry and not even considering that you might have a weapon."

Rick lifted up his T-shirt to expose a flat abdomen dusted with dark golden hair then did a slow pivot, to show her nothing was tucked into the waistband of his jeans. Her breath caught in her throat as she stared at his narrow waist and tight butt. He had a smirky grin on his face when he finished turning, as if he knew exactly what she had been staring at. And why.

He moved toward her. Then stopped, staring at the cookies still cooling on the island. "You bake?" He asked in a voice that was almost reverential.

"Yes. I mean, I used to, but I haven't in a long time. Not much space in Walter Reed or Kandahar for ovens and baking ingredients." She paused, feeling her cheeks heating up with embarrassment, as she moved back to the sink, attempting to look busy and undistracted by starting to wash the dishes. "I baked them for you. For your birthday, yesterday. I mean, I baked them today as a belated birthday present."

"Can I have one now?" He was already reaching for a cookie.

"Yeah, sure. I mean, yes, I think they've cooled enough. Alex and I just sampled one and it was just warm." She licked her lip as if to remove any trace of the cookie she'd eaten. His eyes were immediately drawn to her mouth.

"Can I taste?" The words were a simple request, but his voice was low and husky. He stepped around the island, stopping next to her, their hips touching. Rick reached out and turned her face to his, bending to capture her mouth. Britt gasped at the feel of his tongue sliding between her lips. Frozen in place, her hands still covered with suds, all she could do was sigh as he kissed her like she had never been kissed before. It was possessive and territorial, but it was gentle, too— and arousing as all hell. She moaned, and his fingers slid down to her neck, loosely circling it like a living necklace.

Their mouths still locked together, she tried to turn into his arms, but he blocked her. His body held her in place, one hand on her throat and the other circling her waist and sliding up to cup her breast. One flick of his fingers and her nipple hardened into a diamond tip. She heard him groan against her lips. His cock was a hard rod pressed against her hip. She was achingly aware that only a thin layer of cotton separated her bare skin from his touch. Breaking the kiss, Rick whispered into her ear, his breath a warm arousal.

"Please. Let me. Please, Britt." His hand was sliding into the plunging neckline of her dress, cupping her rounded flesh, his thumb pressing against its center.

"Yes. Yes. Whatever. Just don't stop kissing me." Britt captured his mouth with her own and this time it was her tongue that slid inside. His hand tightened on her breast, kneading it into pleading fullness before he moved to its twin. She felt Rick's other hand sweeping her hemline up and up until her bare hip rested against his denim fly, barely containing his throbbing erection.

"Jesus. God." The words escaped as his mouth pulled away from hers to rain kisses down her neck and onto her shoulder. "Darlin', I've wanted you since I saw you come out of the ocean yesterday morning. Not even knowing who or what you were, I wanted you so bad. But nothing like I want you now, Britt. Tell me it's the same for you. Tell me while I can still stop."

She was melting. She could feel tears gathering in the corners of her eyes, a faint sheen of sweat on her face and her honeyed arousal seeping into her panties. She had never wanted a man so badly. Britt had never thought to desire or need a man again. But, this man, in mere hours, had become the embodiment of everything she had ever sought in a lover, a friend, a comrade-in-arms.

"Yes, oh my god, yes." She almost screamed as his fingers slid into her wetness. A flick of his thumb and she was moaning. The orgasm rocked through her. Rick held her tight with one hand while his fingers fumbled with the fly on his jeans. Hard and hot, his cock pressed against her hip.

"Hurry," She heard herself whisper.

"Your wish is my command." He laughed low and lusty. "Captain."

Rick moved behind her, pushing her panties to the side with one hand while the other continued to play at the apex of her thighs. He bent her slightly over the sink and Britt realized her hands were still deep in the now-cool dish water. She started to giggle but lost all ability to make a sound as she felt his hard length slide into her throbbing passage. He bent her a little more, so her elbows were resting on the edge of the sink. He filled her; she could feel his coarse curls pressing against her ass. He was buried deep. Neither of them moved. The kitchen was filled with their harsh breaths as they both fought for control.

"Jesus, Britt, you're so tight. It feels so good. Damn, I'm not hurting you, am I, darlin'?" She felt Rick start to withdraw and she tightened her pelvic muscles to hold him in place.

"Don't. Don't you dare, Marine. Don't. You. Dare. Stop. Rick." Her voice was one of a command officer.

He laughed and pushed back into her. "That's 'Major', to you, darlin'." And then he began to move. Long, deep strokes of his cock, light flicks from his fingers. She could not be still. Her hips met his every thrust. She felt tremors building inside her again, stronger than before, stronger than she had ever experienced. Just as need overcame her resolve to come with him, she felt him tighten his hold on her hip, holding her in place.

He exploded in her, hard fast thrusts, as he groaned her name. The feel of his passion sent her over the edge. Her head bent forward, resting on her arms, eyes closed, lost in a fantasy that surpassed the most erotic dream she had ever had.

CHAPTER TWELVE

His forehead rested on the nape of her neck. He tried to suck air into lungs that felt like he's just run a marathon. His hands rested on her hips, the thin fabric of her little blue dress bunched under his fingers. Ridiculously, his jeans were bagged around his knees, his boxers not far above them. Rick lifted his head, trying to focus as he looked around her pretty kitchen, steamy with sex. His eyes met the accusing brown ones of her Labrador retriever. Alex was staring at him as if to say, "Make one wrong move and I will sink my teeth into your bare ass."

Laughter rumbled through him, genuine amusement at the ludicrous situation he in which he had put them. Britt raised her head from where it rested on her folded arms. Long strands of silver hair had escaped from her messy little bun and were curled in damp tendrils on her slim neck. She glanced over her shoulder at him. "What is so funny?"

"Look at your dog and smile or I swear he's going to come over here and bite my dick right off."

Britt turned her head toward Alex. His eyes shifted to her with such a look of betrayal that hot red streaks of shame marred her cheeks. "Oh, bugger. He's never seen me with anyone—not like this. Oh, he's going to shame me for a week. Damn."

"I'm sure we can make it up to him. But first, we better get...disentangled." His laughter had caused him to slip from her slick warmth. Rick grabbed the towel Britt had left on the counter and wiped the moisture from between her legs in a matter-of-fact way before he slid her panties back in place and pulled her dress down from where he'd bunched it at her waist. He stepped back slightly and cleaned himself before he got his jeans back up over his hips. "Is your laundry room downstairs?" he asked Britt as he moved away from her.

"No, it's behind that door next to the bathroom, across from the living room."

"I'll toss this towel in the washer. Why don't you get the doggie sentry his favorite treat and we'll attempt to bribe him into not killing me." He sounded only half serious as he strode across the living room. When he returned, Britt was standing in front of the opened door of the refrigerator. The cool air had removed some of the flush from her cheeks, but her lips were swollen and red like ripe cherries.

"I've got an apple, a chunk of cheddar cheese, and a piece of chicken breast." Britt glanced over at Alex then at Rick. "That is one annoyed, hurt, pissed-off dog. I'm going for broke and giving him everything." She pulled the food from the fridge and shut the door with a bump of her hip. Rick felt himself start to harden at the sight of her unconsciously sexy move.

"Let me have the cheese. I think we need to have a man-to-man chat." Rick pulled the cheddar from Britt's hand and walked cautiously toward Alex, never taking his eyes off the dog who now sat at attention in front of the doors to the deck. When Rick reached Alex, he crouched in front of him, holding out the cheese. Almost reluctantly, Alex looked over at Britt, as if seeking approval even though he didn't think she was worthy to command him. She nodded her head slightly. The Lab opened his mouth and the cheese disappeared inside, after a slight nip on Rick's fingertips. He chuckled at the dog's sneak attack then reached out and rubbed the top of Alex's head. "Look, buddy, I know you didn't like witnessing all that, but things got a little out of control. I appreciate you not jumping me. I promise that the next time…" Rick glanced over his shoulder at Britt, who was just staring at him, open-mouthed, before he continued, "if there *is* a next time, I'll be more discreet." He held out his hand to his canine competition. Alex glared at him for a few seconds, then tongue lolling, he lifted his paw for Rick to shake.

Rick stood and ruffled the dog's ears. Turning to Britt, he moved back to the kitchen. "Your turn, Captain. I'd go with the chicken." He opened the refrigerator door. "I need a beer. Can I take one and can I get one out for you?"

"Yes and yes, thank you." Britt eased her way over to Alex who lay on the floor now, his big head resting on his paws, a look of abject sorrow on his face. As Rick leaned against the kitchen counter and opened his beer, Britt sank slowly to floor beside her dog. Her arm went around his neck and she buried her face in his fur. Alex was licking the chicken from Britt's outstretched hand. Rick heard her choked whisper, obviously meant only for the dog.

"I'm sorry. I know what just happened confused and worried you. But, it's okay. I'm okay. See?" She lifted his head in both her hands and was almost nose to nose with the yellow furry face. "I'm fine. It's not like the last time." Rick stepped away from the counter and started to step toward Britt. She held up a hand to stop him, still talking to Alex. "I promised you that would never happen again, and it hasn't. This is different. You have to trust me that this is different." She planted a kiss on his nose. "And I still love you. Forever and ever. You are my guy." Apparently, Alex had decided to forgive her. He licked the back of her hand and sighed before he put his head back down on his paws, his eyes drifting closed.

Rick came to Britt's side and helped her to her feet with one hand under her elbow. He handed her a beer bottle and motioned to the deck. "I think we should take this outside." She didn't ask what he meant. Instead, she nodded her head and motioned for him to follow her. Britt led him across the living room and into her bedroom. He noticed a jumble of ocean colors on the white wicker bed and chair, turquoise and teal curtains framing the glass doors that opened onto the deck. Brit unlatched the door and they stepped out onto a deck area that angled away from the main deck. Two dark blue cushioned chaises sat on the weathered gray planks, a small glass-topped table between them. Britt sank onto the chaise closest to the bedroom door and motioned for Rick to sit on the other. Instead, he nudged her legs over and parked himself so he was facing her. He took a long sip of beer then set his bottle on the little table.

"So, first, let me ask: are you okay?" His eyes searched her pretty but drawn face.

Britt's cheeks flushed a deep rose and she looked away. After a second, she nodded her head and whispered, "I'm okay." Turning her face back toward him, she asked "Are you okay?"

He was taken aback by the concern in her voice. Rick had given himself no thought at all, as worried as he was about the woman and her dog. It took a moment for him to respond. "I'm fine, especially now that I don't have to worry about Alex lying in wait for me, ready to take my leg or some other appendage off in retaliation."

She snickered. "Don't be too sure of that."

Rick did not respond. They sat staring at each other, the silence neither comfortable nor awkward. Two warriors who were used to keeping their thoughts to themselves.

"We need to talk." They both said it at the same time.

Britt waved her hand at him as she took another sip of beer. "You can start."

He groaned. "Ladies first."

She smirked. "You out-rank me. I defer to you, Major."

Stalling, Rick reached for his beer bottle and drew long and hard. He wiped his mouth with the back of his hand. Looking Britt straight in the eye, he began. "In no particular order, let me say first, that that was fantastic. Certainly not the way I thought or hoped we would come together..." He paused as she raised her eyebrows in surprise. "Really? You had to know that something was bound to develop between us, especially after what happened on the beach. I've been wanting you since I first laid eyes on you. That was just a physical reaction to your god damn sexy body. Once I got to know you a little,

I couldn't get you out of my mind. But I didn't come over here tonight to...have sex with you. I just wanted, needed, to see you. I hoped we could talk some more and maybe fool around a little. But then you licked your lip and I was lost."

Her eyes had never left his face. She had a small smile playing about her lips as she listened to him.

"Anyway, I'm not sorry. I just wish I'd handled our first time with a little more finesse. But, it's been awhile...a long while since I was with a woman...and, well, I went off like some green kid. But, I also want to tell you that I'm clean. You don't have to worry about any STDs or anything like that. But, I have to ask, could I have gotten you pregnant?"

She blushed at his question, looking away from him again, her eyes searching for something on the horizon. She shrugged her shoulders and whispered, "No. I mean, probably not." Her fingers were playing nervously with her beer bottle. Her eyes finally met his then skittered away. "The kind of training I went through, the physical demands, it kind of fucks up periods and all. A lot of us women just stopped having them, even after we were deployed. Mine have been iffy for years, but I got birth control shots anyway just to be sure. But, since I was wounded, with the surgeries and all, I haven't had a shot, but I haven't had my period for months, either. I think it's okay. But, maybe, if we do this again, we should, you know, use something."

"Absolutely." He took her hand. "Britt, I'd like to do 'it' again. Like right now." Her eyes opened wide in surprise. He brought her hand to his lips and lightly nipped her palm. "But, I think we need to talk a little more. And I don't want to push you. I know you are still recovering from some serious injuries." Her hands moved to draw the hem of her dress down over her knee. He stopped her. "Don't. You don't have to hide your scars from me. I have plenty of my own. I look at yours and I just see guts and perseverance. You should be proud of them."

"Are you proud of yours?" Her question gave him pause. He shrugged, uncomfortable with any answer he might give to her.

"I don't really think about them much anymore. It's been a long time." It was his turn to look away, his gaze straying up the shore, where lights were starting to come on. His voice was strained when he turned back to her.

"Look, I don't do this. I mean, I don't get involved. I don't have much emotion left to offer." He shook his head, at a loss for words. This time, Britt reached for his hand. He made to draw it away, but her slim hand was surprisingly strong, and she held on.

"So, you're a 'wham, bam, thank you ma'am', kind of guy? Is that what you're trying to tell me? Funny, I didn't figure you for the 'love 'em and leave 'em' type." He couldn't tell if she was serious or just baiting him.

"I'm not. I just leave. Love doesn't factor into the equation."

"I see, so this is just a 'summer at the beach' thing. You'll be gone in September? Isn't there an old song about that?"

"I don't know if it will last the summer or not. I just leave when it's time to leave. Or when I get called back into it."

"You can't say no? You can't say thank you. I've served, I'm done? Or don't you want to?"

"I want to *now*. After this last shit storm, I *want* to say no. But, sometimes, it suits my purpose to leave and I can blame it on Uncle Sam." He ran his fingers through his hair. "I've never told a woman that before."

"Rick, you can come and go, I have no expectations. I'm just trying to get back into shape and decide what I want to do next with my life. I was fine here before you arrived. I'll be fine when you go."

His cheeks grew warm with embarrassment. "Well, damn. That's usually my line."

"I think we may be more alike than you know." She said it with a small smile.

He realized that he thought her smile was the sweetest thing he'd seen in a long time. How did such a lovely woman end up in the middle of such an ugly war?

"What did you mean when you said to Alex this was not like the last time?"

She started at his question, dropping his hand back in his lap. She

76

started to move off the chaise. He laid a hand on her leg. "Tell me. We're telling truths out here, tonight. Tell me."

Rick could feel her withdraw from him although she physically moved no farther away. She stilled and stiffened, sitting up straighter and drawing into herself. A long, low sigh escaped her lips. He waited what seemed like forever for her to begin speaking. When she did, her smile was gone. Her voice was flat, almost emotionless, like she was reading a report.

"It was in Afghanistan. You know how it is there. Way more men than women. There had been a few times in the past when I was involved with someone on base. A doctor in a hospital where I was stationed in the States. An Air Force pilot in Germany. But never anyone in my unit, never anyone I worked with every day. But we were all thrown together in Kandahar. And there were only a couple of women attached to the Rangers. I got assigned to his unit. He was already there, it was his second tour. We were only on maneuvers together once in a while. I didn't get sent out unless the target likely had women and children who would need to be contained and questioned. But we had a lot in common. We were both from Ohio, career Army, had enlisted after 9/11. And there was Alex. The unit had adopted him as a pup, right before I was deployed. I fell in love with that dog the moment I saw him. And I was on base more than some of the others, I had clinical duties involving civilians, so we were together most of the time. It got so Alex was sleeping in my quarters. But this officer had been the one who found him, he named him. So, he took to stopping by to see how Alex was doing."

Britt fell silent. Her bottle of beer was empty. Rick handed his beer to her and she drained it. He could tell she was uncomfortable but he had to know, so he nudged her leg as a signal to continue.

"Well, I'm sure you've seen stuff like this before. Things happen. We were spending a lot of time together. I didn't realize that he—that he was thinking of me in a physical way. I didn't see it coming. One night, we were in my quarters, sitting on my bunk, Alex was snoozing on his blanket in the corner. The guy made a move on me, pushed me down on the bed, got his hands all over me, before I could react. I was

77

pushing him off me, telling him no, I wasn't interested. And Alex jumped on him, sank his teeth into his shoulder. This asshole sat up, shoving Alex so hard he went flying across the room. But that moved him off me, so I was able to get up and run to Alex. I got on the floor with him and began yelling at the guy to get out. A few other female officers came to the door to see what was going on. He was yelling that the dog went crazy and attacked him without provocation. I just kept holding Alex and telling the man to leave. He finally stomped off, in a real tantrum. He filed a complaint. Fortunately, a couple of the other women came forward with me and made statements that Alex was only trying to protect me from this guy's unwanted advances. That was pretty much the end of it. We got to keep Alex in our quarters and I didn't go out on any other operations with him."

Rick sat watching her, nodding to her that he understood. But he didn't. There was something not right with this story. But he was not going to pursue it. Not yet.

CHAPTER THIRTEEN

She should be sound asleep. After the physical and emotional events of the day, Britt figured she would be passed out once she climbed into bed after kissing Rick goodnight on the deck outside her bedroom. But there she was, at three o'clock in the morning, staring through her door at a mid-summer moon casting a silvery swath across the ocean. Alex's butt was pressed up against hers, his doggy snores competing with the sound of waves brushing the shore and Britt's exasperated sighs.

Rick had not bought her story, not entirely. She was certain of that even though she had told him the truth about the incident in Afghanistan, every word she told him was the truth. Just not the complete truth. She was not ready for that—she would probably never be ready to reveal the entire story of her tour of duty in Afghanistan.

Alex stirred in his sleep, turning over and resting his big head on her hip. She reached down to pet him and was rewarded with a warm lick along her hand. Thank god for this dog—truly her family.

"Buddy, you did so good tonight. You know Rick is a good guy and we have nothing to fear from him. I'm a little embarrassed you had to witness that fuckfest in the kitchen." Giggling, she could feel herself blushing—blushing at the memories of Rick's mouth and hands on her. It had been a long, long, time since she had been kissed, hugged, or held. Even longer since the last time she'd had sex. The past two years had been brutal. Nine months of combat in the unique hell that was Kandahar followed by fifteen months of surgeries, rehabilitation, physical therapy, more surgeries, more rehab, and then the last few months of trying to figure out who she was and what she wanted. Her aunt and uncle's offer of their beach cottage for the summer had been a godsend.

It was supposed to be a time for relaxation and reflection. Britt had arrived in April with two suitcases, one trunk, and a big yellow dog that had only recently been flown from Afghanistan to America. The one bright spot in all those months had been the news that she could have Alex, that a private animal adoption agency would arrange for him to come to the United States. That in itself was almost a miracle. Alex had not been a military canine; like so many other strays, he had been found rooting around in the garbage near the base in Kandahar. And like so many other dogs, he had been adopted by the unit to which Britt had been assigned. It helped that the soldier who found and named Alex was a Lieutenant Colonel in charge of the Battalion that included Britt's company. And that was the start of Britt's trouble.

Lt. Colonel Jonathan "Jake" Gable was the epitome of a soldier's soldier. West Point grad, decorated, tall, dark, and handsome and with a line of bullshit that impressed the brass, played well to the press, and had women swooning. Except Jake wasn't satisfied with just the women who wanted him—he was particularly interested in the women who did not succumb to his "charms." Like Britt, like a sergeant in administration, like an operating room lieutenant and who knew how many other women he had forced into bed and bullied into silence.

Britt sat up and swung her legs over the side of the bed. Alex stirred but did not wake up. She grabbed a quilt from the end of the bed and quietly made her way out onto the deck. The temperature was still summer night warm, but the ocean breeze was cool. Wrapping herself in the soft cotton coverlet, she curled up on the chaise and dealt once again with the demons in her head.

If she was telling the truth to herself, she had known on some level that Jake's interest in her was more than just professional. At first, it had been easy to attribute his attentiveness to their shared affection for Alex. But, as she looked back, there had been signs. And she knew those signs. No woman who had risen through the ranks, who had served in combat units, who had navigated her way through the military for almost twenty years would have been surprised by Jake's moves. Britt had chosen to ignore them and deal with him in a professional manner while they were on duty and with what she hoped he would see as simple camaraderie the rest of the time.

Men like Jake weren't looking for camaraderie, they were looking for conquests. As Britt huddled down into the quilt, she admitted she had been hoping his interest in her would wane before she had to confront him or, worse, go over his head to his superior officer. A sob tore from her throat as she recalled how that had gone. After the attack in her quarters, Britt had filed a written report with her commander. She probably would have kept quiet if it had only been her, she now realized, but she had to save Alex from being destroyed. And the sergeant and the operating room nurse had come to her and related their own experiences with Jake's harassment. Safety in numbers, they naively believed.

The upshot had been that command had decided Alex was no threat to the unit and could remain on base, under Britt's care. The quid pro quo was that there was no "official" record of the event, nothing in Jake's file about his predilection for preying on women working with or under him. Britt had been unwilling to accept the result, even though it meant saving Alex, but the other two women had urged her to do so. It was apparent nothing was really going to be done to the slick Lieutenant Colonel and they all felt they had gotten all they could hope for by being able to keep Alex in their quarters. And verbal assurances that they would not be assigned to work with or near Jake.

Britt's days in Afghanistan had continued without contact from

Jake until the fateful night when two women assigned to the team were still recovering from minor injuries suffered on a previous night mission, which mean that Britt and Nadia were needed to replace them. Information had come in that a tribal leader who had been eluding them for months had been spotted in a village about an hour's flight away. As he and his men were believed to be encamped in a large family compound in the village, Britt and her translator would be needed to isolate and interrogate the women and children who were living there.

"Not a problem," Britt had answered when she got the call. It had been almost a week since she had been out on patrol and she was almost looking forward to getting off the base and seeing some action.

Her willingness to proceed faltered when she saw who was leading the mission. Jake was suited up and heading for the other chopper when Britt and Nadia arrived on the tarmac. He did not go out on many missions, but he obviously was eager to be in on bagging the elusive Taliban leader. "Well, damn," she had muttered to Nadia. "Maybe we'll be lucky, and we won't have any contact with him." Nadia had shrugged and grinned at Britt; they had been pretty lucky so far.

Their luck ran out that night. It was several weeks before Britt was able to piece together what had happened. After the blast, she had been out of it on drugs for the flight back to Kandahar, heavily medicated at the base hospital, and then sedated for the flight to Germany. There had been two surgeries, one to reconstruct her knee and the other to repair the damage to her shoulder caused by the shrapnel. Then, a third operation a few days later to deal with complications in her knee. In between, she'd been questioned about the mission. She gave her best recollection of the events of that night and thought the inquiry was over.

About a month later, while still at Landstuhl, she had been called upon to answer more questions. Questions about why she had not called for support once she realized she and Nadia were at risk. Britt had told her story again and again, that she had called command to report there were insurgents approaching and then again when she heard them outside the room where she and Nadia had been with the women. "Why do you keep asking me? Of course, I called for assistance. We could hear them outside the door. Nadia told me the woman was yelling to the men that there were American soldiers in the room and to come in and kill us. I got no answer both times I called."

Then she heard the awful lie. The commander had said there was no call. That she was known as a maverick who thought she could take on any number of enemy fighters on her own. The commander was Jake. Britt just shut down. The next few months were a blur of medication and painful physical therapy. She went through the painful exercises because she was ordered to do so. She talked to no one, basically refused to meaningfully participate in any counseling, just waited to see if she was going to be dishonorably discharged. Or worse.

She was eventually transferred to Walter Reed to learn to walk again with a knee that was full of metal, plastic and cadaver bone. And, given her depression, for some psychiatric counseling. They all thought it was PTSD and she was sure that was some of it. But, it was grieving for Nadia. She had lost her closest friend and comrade that night. She had lost her dog, too, as Alex was still in Kandahar, being cared for by her unit. But, she had been betrayed by the Army and that was a pain that no drugs and no therapy could heal.

Despite her disinterest, she healed. At least physically. Ready to be discharged from the hospital, she had been interviewed one last time. She would be honorably discharged for medical reasons; obviously, given her injuries she was no longer fit for active duty. And she was being awarded the Bronze Star for her actions that night and a Purple Heart. Despite her questions, the only official answer she received was that further inquiry had shown that she did call in for assistance and that troops had been dispatched to her and Nadia. But they arrived too late. No one was at fault. Britt accepted the discharge and the citations—there was nothing else to do. She resolved to put the whole experience behind her and move forward.

Roused out of her depression, she had reached out to her former unit to ask about having Alex sent to the States. Surprisingly, the process moved along smoothly and quickly. She wondered what gods were looking out for her. She found she desperately wanted to have her dog back, her one happy connection to her time in Afghanistan. Then she got a letter from the sergeant who had stood with her against Jake. It seemed the inquiry into the incident the night Britt had been injured and Nadia killed had finally revealed that Jake, when he heard it was Britt requesting assistance, had laughed and said, "Another hysterical female. I don't know why they put them in combat. They're only good for one thing." It was not until her second call that he had reluctantly ordered some men "to go see what was scaring the ladies." Jake had been reassigned Stateside, he would not command a combat battalion again. That was it.

Tears streaming down her face, Britt sat watching the sun start to peek over the horizon. It was a good thing Rick was a temporary fling, at best. He'd be off in the wind at some point, probably before he became suspicious enough about the holes in the stories she had told him about "the guy" and "that night" to ask her some tough questions. And, given who he was and what he knew about the military, Britt was certain it would not take Rick long to start putting the pieces together. From the look on his face when she told him her story, she knew Rick would get all knight-in-shining-armor and try to avenge her honor.

"Damn," she caustically laughed at the rising sun, "I would not want to be Lieutenant Colonel Jake Gable if Rick ever gets his hands on him. But I would surely love to see it."

CHAPTER FOURTEEN

He'd slept well enough, Rick figured, dragging his hands across his haggard face as he stared in the mirror at a man who looked way older than 51. After an early morning, a daring beach rescue, a sexy as all hell romantic encounter at the kitchen sink and a desperately inadequate tale about an asshole Lieutenant Colonel, a gutsy Captain and a fierce guard dog, he should probably still be asleep. But his internal alarm clock went off at six o'clock every damn morning, whether he'd gotten eight hours of sleep or two. Last night he had tossed and turned, haunted by erotic dreams of Britt and violent images of pounding the damn guy who had molested her into a bloody pulp. And running though all of that, was the nagging worry he was missing something.

He dressed for a run on the beach and took off down the shore like a man on a mission. An hour later, he climbed the steps to his deck, sweaty and breathing hard. He'd thought he saw Britt curled up on the chaise on the deck outside her bedroom door when he had started, but now all that was left on the chaise was a bunched-up blanket. The curtains over the door to her bedroom were still closed. Before he jumped in the shower, he sent a text to Mick: *Meet me at the diner in thirty minutes.* His phone beeped as he was toweling off: *What the fuck? I'll be there.*

The Jeep was coated with a light dusting of sand when he hopped in. *Looks like I've just driven it through Afghanistan. Or Iraq. Or fucking Syria.* He was so sick of sand-encrusted vehicles that he vowed to wash the damn Jeep as soon as he finished breakfast with Mick.

When he entered the diner, he immediately saw Mick in the corner booth, hunched over a big white mug of steaming coffee. An identical mug sat across from him. Rick slid onto the seat opposite his old friend. Mick didn't even look up. He took a long sip of coffee and muttered, "I'm eating a fucking pound of bacon this morning. Just so you know. My girls made me overnight oatmeal to have today." He looked up at Rick. "That damn shit is cold. Cold oatmeal! I felt like I was back in Bosnia!"

Rick was chuckling at his buddy's distress as he wrapped his hands around the thick stoneware cup. His laughter ceased when he saw the knowing look Mick was sending him.

"What?" Rick thought to forestall the inevitable interrogation by playing dumb.

"Cut the shit. You want me to meet you at the diner this early? You didn't sleep last night, it's all over your face, even though I bet you had your skinny ass up at dawn pounding the beach running? What did you do? Five miles? Fifty? I never saw a man run from emotional turmoil like you, bro. You'd run headfirst into battle with nothing but a knife between your teeth. But let anyone or anything get near that chunk of ice in your chest, and you take flight. Is it your ex-wife, the red-haired lawyer, or the wounded warrior that has you all messed up?" Having finished his tirade, Mick leaned back against the cracked red leather of the booth's upholstery and glared at him.

Rick started to protest but the words died on his tongue. "It's Britt. And I'm not running away from her. But, I'm scared shitless."

The bald honesty of the statement brought a raised eyebrow from Mick. It was not as though Rick had made such an admission before. Mick knew about most of the women who had come into and then quickly exited Rick's life. Rick knew Mick had high hopes for the lawyer last autumn, but Rick had gotten spooked and taken off to see his son before he'd lost himself in the backwaters of Southeast Asia and the Middle East, by way of Afghanistan.

"I really like her, and I think she likes me. Her dog sort of likes me and I am no longer living in fear of him biting me in the ass, though he had me down in the surf yesterday like a beached whale." That last got a laugh from Mick. A waitress delivered two gigantic breakfast platters, with an extra side of bacon. The two men chatted about their kids while she topped off their coffee mugs and hovered around to see if they wanted anything else. Assured that they were fine, she moved slowly away.

"She's giving you the eye, old man." Rick pointed at Mick with a crispy strip of bacon, before popping it into his mouth.

"Bullshit. She was batting those eyelashes at you, you dumb fuck. No wonder you can't seem to get a woman to stay with you. You can't read their signals for shit." Mick dug into the rapidly shrinking mountain of bacon. The two men attacked their breakfast platters like it was their last meal. A few moments later, Rick picked up the conversation.

"I read the signals just fine, Mick. That's the problem. I think I may be reading too much into every word Britt says." He pushed his plate away and wiped traces of bacon grease from his mouth before tossing his napkin down on the table.

"What do you mean?" Mick gave up on his breakfast too.

"Well, here's the deal. Britt and I have been talking about how we came to be on the Shore this summer. She told me some stuff about how she was injured by a grenade in a compound in Afghanistan while she was attached to a Rangers' unit. Messed up her knee really bad, took some shrapnel in her shoulder and had a mother of a concussion. They patched her up at Kandahar, sent her to Landstuhl, and eventually, she ended up at Walter Reed. Bunch of surgeries, some PT, some rehab. Probably some psych therapy, too. She was released a few months ago, took a medical discharge, and ended up next door to my place in Bill and Carole's cottage—they're her aunt and uncle."

"Jesus, that's a hell of a tale. Sounds like she was damn lucky to

survive that mess. An injury like that gets infected and you're done."
Mick grew silent. "Remember that guy in Iraq?" Mick shook his head
at the memory of a comrade who had died in Germany after taking
the blast from an IED.

"Yeah. She was lucky. Sort of. It all sounds pretty by-the-book, the
way she tells it. Only, her translator—another woman in her unit—
gets killed, taking most of the blast. Britt's still dealing with that...like
anyone would...like we've done. You're in charge of an op and one of
your team gets dead taking the shot meant for you. You deal with it.
But it sucks." Rick leaned forward, his voice dropping.

"But here's the thing: Britt called in for assistance once she knew
there were insurgents surrounding her location. She had two units at
least of fucking Rangers—and those guys aren't pussies—who were in
the compound with the women, and no one responds to her call. And
no one comes to their aid? That's bullshit."

Mick nodded. "But, you know, maybe they were under fire, too,
and couldn't respond as fast because they were pinned down." Mick's
voice trailed off as if he knew it was a weak-ass excuse.

"Maybe. But she didn't say that. She didn't say anything more
about the incident than what I told you. So, okay, maybe she doesn't
like to talk about it. We also know how that is. But, last night she lets
slip that some *guy* in her unit or battalion hit on her at Kandahar.
Some guy she thought was only interested in the dog."

Mick snorted in disbelief.

"Yeah, I know, a woman looks like Britt, has a brain and guts, too.
And she thinks a guy only wants to hang around with her because he
likes Alex. I mean, that dog *is* pretty cool but, seriously, no. I call bullshit on that." Rick just shook his head at the absurdity of Britt's
unawareness of her appeal to men. To him.

"Did you tell her that?" Disbelief was evident in Mick's voice.

"No, I just mostly listened. Seems Alex jumped the guy when he got
too handy with Britt one night and the guy threw him against the wall.
Then, when Britt started yelling at him and some of her bunkmates
came to the door, he blamed it on Alex. He claims the dog attacked him

and he was acting in self-defense. The asshole files a complaint against the dog but Britt and her friends speak up and the complaint is thrown out and they get to keep Alex in their quarters. And Britt says she never got assigned to go on a mission with the cocksucker dickwad guy again."

"Really?" Mick drew the word out, his voice emphasizing just how little faith he placed in the truth of that statement.

"Yeah, I know. *Really?* What I think is that the asshole was on duty that night Britt was injured, and her friend was killed. I think he might even have been in command. And we both know that I know just how to find out who this son of a bitch is. And just how to deal with him."

"Wait a minute, bro. You go behind her back and start looking at her records—because that is what you'll have to do to track this jerk down—and she finds out? You will be toast. She'll burn you for that. You know it."

"So, I'm supposed to let this *guy* get away with this shit? A woman was killed because she and Britt didn't get back-up from their team. Britt's probably never going to be able to walk properly again. That's not right, man, that is just not right."

"No, it's not. But it's her decision to make and her battle to fight and you can't come riding in to save the day like some knight in fucking armor. Don't do it, Rick. This woman looks like she could be a keeper. Don't fuck it up." Mick reached over and grabbed Rick's hand. "Don't blow this."

Looking Mick in the eye, all Rick could promise was, "I'll think about it. I'll think on it a little more, man. That's all."

"That's enough." Mick drank the last of his coffee. "I'll pay the damn bill because even though you rousted me out of bed too fucking early, at least you saved me from god damn cold oatmeal."

After finding a car wash and cleaning the inside and outside of the Jeep, Rick spent some time driving up and down Long Beach Island, trying to sort out his thoughts. He'd seen the wisdom in Mick's advice to wait before trying to track down the asshole who had made Britt's life miserable in Kandahar. That didn't mean he wasn't going to do a little snooping online. And it also didn't mean he wasn't going to try to get more of the story from Britt.

But he had a more immediate concern to deal with before he saw Britt again. Something he could not discuss with anyone, even Mick. He pulled into a public beach parking lot in Surf City and just sat, staring out at the ocean. The foam as the waves broke on the shore reminded him of the suds that Britt's hands had been buried in when he'd pulled her to him last night and finally kissed her the way he'd wanted to from the very first. He'd felt that kiss in every fiber of his being. And he was getting hard just remembering how good it had felt to be buried deep in her warm, wet, pussy.

That was the problem. He had just had sex with a woman in a way he hadn't experienced in years. He was always in control—he set the pace, he decided when, where, and how. He wasn't tender, and he was never a supplicant. Not that he ever forced any woman, ever. That was a line never to be crossed. He made his wishes known, he never pleaded. Yet, he'd practically begged Brit to let him have her. And it was just about the best sex he'd ever had.

It had been years, pretty much since with his wife Elizabeth, since he'd had sex with a woman when he was not in control—when the focus of his love-making was not all about control. And where he desperately needed there to be pain with pleasure. Where restraints, some biting and spanking, and his unquestioned authority were part and parcel of intimacy. Nothing gentle or tender, nothing that resembled love. It had not always been that way for him; his need for control had evolved over time after his first marriage ended. He figured it was a defense mechanism for guarding his heart. Then, after years of watching good men and women die or get totally fucked up, it also became a way to ensure the safety of his partners. If he controlled every aspect of their lovemaking, nothing bad would happen. No one would get hurt. It was less a need to dominate a submissive woman than it was his need to dominate the situation.

Unbelievably, the previous night, he'd exercised virtually no control. He hadn't even used a rubber, for christsake. Rick sat in his Jeep, gazing at the Atlantic but not really seeing it. He was envisioning

Britt on that big white bed of hers, spread out naked, writhing, wanting pain with her pleasure. She was game, he'd give her that. She was a tough warrior, used to being in a command position, used to leading and not following, courageous and resilient. He doubted she would be able to hand over control, even if just in the bedroom, to him.

The stiff wind was stirring up the ocean, creating whitecaps as far as he could see. The sun was burning down on him and he realized that it was approaching noon. The morning had disappeared while he was daydreaming about a woman he couldn't quite wrap his mind around. But, it came to him that he didn't begrudge the time he'd spent thinking about Britt. As he started up the Jeep and pulled away from the beach, he caught his reflection in the rear-view mirror. He was grinning.

CHAPTER FIFTEEN

It felt so damn good to just lie in the sun. A cool breeze off the Atlantic kept Britt from burning up and so did the huge mug of lemonade on the table next to her. Across the deck, in the shade, Alex had been snoozing on the other chaise since their post-breakfast swim. They'd rinsed off under the outdoor shower then stretched out on towels draped over the chaise lounges to let the sun dry them off. Britt had stripped off her swim T-shirt and knife and covered herself with sunscreen—especially her still-healing wounds. The cluster on her shoulder was fading to pink but the huge scar that ran across her knee was still a deep red.

Looking down at the evidence of her last operation as she sat up in order to flip over onto her belly, she chuckled. "Damn scar is almost the same color as my swimsuit. Matchy-matchy as Aunt Susan would say." Her aunt was known for coordinating everything. Brit and her mom had often laughed about Aunt Susan's almost compulsive need to color-coordinate her nail color, jewelry and even her underwear with her clothes. She even wrapped gifts in the same colors as the contents of the package. And she always seemed surprised when Britt would mention the color of her present before she even opened it, just by looking at the bow. Smiling, she thought if that was her aunt's only vice—and it was—it was a harmless and often amusing one.

It's been a long time coming, Mom, but at least I can smile at my memories of you, now. You were right—time heals all wounds. It's just that some take longer than others. Britt reached up to rub the twinge in her shoulder. A dull noise off to her left caused her to lift her head. Rick had just plopped a large galvanized tub on his deck. Britt silently stared at him, appreciating the play of muscles across his back, his strong arms and, as he turned, his very nice tight ass. Before she even gave it a thought, Britt pursed her lips and let out a long, low wolf whistle. Rick's head whipped around in her direction. His eyes widened when he realized the whistle had come from her. Britt just grinned. Today she felt so damn good. She shouldn't—she hadn't gotten much sleep after her all-night reverie and her shoulder was sore from a too vigorous swim, but her muscles were loose, the sun was shining, and the very gorgeous man who had fucked her senseless last night was staring appreciatively at her from just a few feet away.

She propped herself up on her elbows and pushed her sunglasses up into her hair.

Rick ambled over to the edge of his deck, grinning too. "Hey, neighbor. How you doin' today?"

"I'm doing fine. Had a late morning swim with that lazy yellow dog, now snoring over there in the shade, and I'm just lying here in the sun, sipping my lemonade and dreaming about lunch."

"I just picked up some hoagies when I stopped for beer and ice. I'm happy to share. You want Italian cold cuts or tuna salad?"

"You have to stop feeding me. I feel guilty about not cooking for you."

"You made salad the first night and you baked me cookies last night." He stopped speaking and just stared intently at her. She'd bet he was remembering how he got his first taste of those cookies: from her lips. And she could feel her already flushed cheeks heat up even more from the memory. Her nipples tightened, and her insides quivered. She reached out for a sip of her frosty lemonade to cool down and wet her throat enough, so she could speak.

"Ahem. I'll have tuna, thank you very much. Would you like some lemonade? It's homemade."

"Homemade? Yes, ma'am. You want to eat here or over there?"

"Alex is still sleeping, why don't you come over? Just bring the sandwiches, I'll get plates and stuff when I go get your lemonade." She rose from the chaise, reaching behind to pull the bottom of the suit down a little farther over her ass. Rick stopped with his mouth actually hanging open for a moment. Britt glanced down and realized her nipples were plainly visible, pushing against the tight red fabric of her swimsuit. Though her first instinct was to hunch or fold her arms across her chest, she surprised herself by standing even straighter. Laughing, she called out, "Damn wind is colder than I thought." Rick's amused chuckle followed her into the cottage.

"Brazen hussy," she scolded herself. Where had that sexy bravado come from? It had been a long, long time since she'd flirted with a man. "And I used to be damn good at it, too." Within a few moments, she put together a tray of plates, napkins, a pile of cookies, and an iced mug of lemonade for Rick. Dashing into her bedroom, she found the short red, white, and blue striped cover-up her aunt had bought to match her red tank suit. Pulling it on over her head, she was just emerging from the cottage when Rick stepped onto her deck. He had the wrapped sandwiches and a bag of chips in his arms. And a bottle of gin.

At her raised eyebrow, he smirked and said "My grandmother always loved gin and pink lemonade in the summer. The minute you said lemonade, I thought of that. And her." Placing his goodies on the table, he leaned over and kissed her cheek. "Thank you for that memory."

It was all she could do to keep from rubbing her fingers along her face, to feel the kiss again. Instead, she busied herself with arranging the dishes on the table. Just as they sat down, Alex lifted his sleepy head and yawned. The sight of food galvanized him and within seconds he had plopped on the deck between them, head swiveling from one to the other, as if challenging them to see who could feed him first.

"I'm not giving him any tuna salad." Brit stated as she bit into her sandwich. "Mayonnaise gives him gas."

Rick was already pulling pieces of roast beef from the interior of his sandwich. "He can have roast beef, right?"

Britt nodded and added some chips to the little pile Rick was making for her dog. As they ate, they took turns dropping a piece of meat or a chip into Alex's open mouth. Laughing at the dog's antics filled any awkward pauses in their conversation.

After finishing his sandwich, Rick opened the bottle of gin, adding a good shot to his lemonade glass. Looking at Britt, he held the bottle over her glass. When she nodded, he did the same for her.

"Cheers!" He tapped his mug against hers and took a long sip. She followed suit.

"Mmmm. Good combination! I've had gin and tonic before but not gin and lemonade. It's delicious."

"It has to be good gin and homemade lemonade to do the trick. Least that's what Grandma Nellie always said."

"Was she you mom's mom or your dad's mom?" Britt took another sip of the icy concoction.

"Nellie was my mother's mother. Nell West Sheridan. She brought me up." At Britt's raised eyebrows, he continued. "My mom was her oldest daughter. A wild one. She went off to college and got pregnant her sophomore year. She didn't tell my grandmother who the father was; my Aunt Susan, who was four years younger than my mother, told me it was because she didn't know. Anyway, she came home to have me that summer before her junior year at UAlbany. My grandmother offered to take care of me—so my mother could go back to school, finish her teaching degree, and graduate. The deal was that she was to come home to Cambridge—that's a little town north of Albany and east of Saratoga...."

Britt smiled enigmatically, murmuring "I know where it is."

Rick seemed surprised by her admission, but she was not going to elaborate. Not then. She motioned her hand for him to continue. She'd told him part of her story, she wanted to hear more about him before she shared any more details of her life.

"She—my mother's name was Ellen—was supposed to come home every weekend to be with me and help out my grandmother. And she did for most of her junior year. But she never came home at the end of spring semester. All my grandmother heard was that she had packed up her car and left after her exams, saying she was headed home. Ellen died in a car crash in Ohio on July third, the day before my first birthday. She was *not* headed back East."

Tears stung Britt's eyes at the thought of a young boy who never got to know his mother, who had suffered such a tremendous loss at such a tender age. She reached out for Rick's hand, brought it to her lips for a soft kiss. His eyes widened at her emotional response. But he didn't pull his hand away.

"So, my grandmother had custody of me and from then on it was me, Susan, and Nell. My grandfather had passed away pretty young, working on the railroad. Using the insurance money, my grandmother had purchased a two-story building on the main street of Cambridge and opened an antique shop. There was an apartment upstairs where she lived with my aunt and my mother. A small lawn and garden in the back. That's where I grew up."

Taking another sip of his drink, Rick paused in his story. He sat looking out to sea, as if she wasn't even there. But, he didn't move his hand away from Britt's.

"We did okay. Actually, we did better than okay. I don't remember ever wanting for anything. Except a convertible when I was in high school. I didn't think driving the store's delivery van was too cool. But, by then, my Aunt Susan was married to my Uncle Theodore. As long as I took my cousins, Colleen and Maggie, out on a Saturday afternoon for a movie or some of their never-ending lessons, I could use his car for Saturday night dates. It was a pretty good deal. Especially when he got a baby blue Cadillac my senior year in high school. Man, I loved that car. When I went off to college, they gave me my aunt's Honda. It was a generous gift and a good car, but, oh, baby, I lusted after that Caddy." He laughed and winked at Britt. "It was a great make-out car!"

She laughed, too, but her breath caught in her throat at the image of a young Rick in the wide backseat of a big car, trying to have his way with some smitten young woman. Britt smiled to herself at the secret knowledge that she probably would have put out for him.

Rick had turned his hand under hers, now grasping it. A sly smile played across his face as he began tugging on her hand, pulling her up and out of the chair.

"What the hell?" She sputtered the question as his other hand reached out for her. In seconds she was plopped down on his lap, acutely aware that she was sitting on a very aroused male.

"Wanna make out?" Rick nuzzled her neck, nipping lightly at her throat.

A small moan escaped her lips. His hands tightened on hers, holding them pressed into her thighs. Britt was starting to squirm, the thin fabric of her swimsuit providing almost no barrier between his growing erection and her dampening crotch. His tongue trailed kisses up her throat to her ear, while she tried to twist her head, so she could capture his mouth with her own. He nudged her head away, so he could reach her bare shoulder, licking at the exposed skin, warmed by the sun and getting hotter under his ministrations.

"I want to kiss you; why won't you kiss me?" Britt almost moaned the words.

"I've kissed you already. I just wanted to explore more of your sexy body. With my mouth." He planted a noisy kiss on her collarbone. "And with my teeth," he said while nipping at her ear. "And with my fingers." Suddenly, he released her hands and drew them behind her back, where he held them loosely with one of his own. His other hand was in her hair, pulling her face closer to his.

She was imprisoned in Rick's embrace, but she didn't feel threatened. Instead, she leaned into him to savor the kiss. Her tongue flicked out to touch his lip. He drew back for an instant, his eyes searching hers, then he penetrated her mouth in one sweeping thrust.

Britt was writhing on his lap as he deepened the kiss. It was like being devoured by a force of nature. She wanted to wrap her arms around his neck, but she couldn't get loose from his iron grip. But as soon as she began pulling against his hold, he released her. Within seconds, her arms were wrapped around Rick's neck, kissing him as deeply as she could.

He broke the embrace His hands cradled her face. "Darlin', if you don't want me to lay you down on that chaise over there and make love to you in front of your dog and that very nice family having the picnic down on the beach, we better slow down."

Britt laid her lips against his again, briefly. Her need emboldened her. "My bedroom is just through that door over there," she said, nodding her head toward the area where they had been sitting last night. She started to rise, but he stopped her.

"I'm in no condition to stand just this minute, Captain." He glanced down at his lap with a rueful smile. She had to grin, too. "And I think we should talk a bit more first." His words and the look in his eyes wiped the smile from her face.

CHAPTER SIXTEEN

"Wrong choice of words, maybe, darlin'. Just sit back down and listen to what I have to say." Rick patted the seat next to him.

Britt dropped rigidly into the chair, with a doubtful look on her face. And steel in her spine.

He ran both hands through his hair, buying a few seconds, trying to find the right words. "I'm out of my element here, darlin'...."

She interrupted him, command in her voice. "If we're talking about intimate details here, I'd prefer if you used my name, so at least I know this is not some pat speech that you've given to a hundred women before."

Oh, Christ. I am totally fucking this up. He needed to get the right words out, but his vocabulary had disappeared. All he could think about was pulling off that scrap of a red bathing suit and burying his cock deep within her hot, welcoming depths.

"God, Britt, I really want to fuck you. I hardly slept last night. I've been thinking about you all morning. I got hard the minute I walked out on my deck and saw you." He stopped as a smart-ass grin split her face.

"Well, then why did you stop me from dragging you into my bedroom a few minutes ago and having my way with you?"

He choked the words out. "Because...because, Britt, women don't have their way with me. I don't allow it. To use your words, I have my way with them."

She wasn't grinning but at least she wasn't frowning. Confusion swam in her eyes and her lips were parted as if to ask him a question, but what question? She sat even straighter as realization wiped the confusion from her eyes.

"What, what are you saying? You...what? You can't mean you force women?" She rose abruptly, then just stood, swaying. "I couldn't have been that wrong about you. Not...again."

Rick stood, too, and wrapped the stiff, unyielding woman in a gentle embrace. She didn't give an inch. "No, no, darlin'. Britt. I don't force women. I never have. Only a lousy cocksucking cur would rape a woman. No, I don't force women, but I do control them."

"You mean, like BDSM? You're a Dom and you want women to be submissive? Is that it?" She had a skeptical look on her face, but at least she had relaxed a little. Then she whispered, "Like *Fifty Shades of Gray*? Like with handcuffs and riding crops?" He felt her nipples harden against his chest.

Rick moved away from her a little, so he could see her face. *God, she is beautiful.* Silvery blonde hair loosened by the stiff breeze was blowing around her sea-blue eyes and her full lips. He glanced down her body, reacting instantly to her long, lean legs and her full breasts, her nipples clearly visible beneath the swimsuit and thin cover-up. Britt was eyeing him with suspicion and...interest.

"I'm no damn Christian Gray. He's young enough to be my son and a million times richer. I don't do BDSM, Britt. But I need to control... the situation. And I need to know you will do as I say."

She plopped back down into the chair with a sharp laugh. "Well, then we're at a stalemate, Major. I stopped taking orders from any man, from anyone, when I signed my discharge papers." She looked up at him with sadness in her eyes. "It's too bad, Rick. I was really starting to like you. And Alex likes you. And, well, the sex last night was pretty damn amazing for me. Like, the best ever." Her voice caught, and she looked away. "I'm sorry it wasn't the same for you. That you feel the need to tell me to do it...differently."

"You're wrong." Rick returned to his chair and reached out for her hands. "It was pretty much the best sex I ever had, too. And I can't get my head around it. From my experience for the last twenty years or so, I should have had your hands pinned behind your back, your nipples red and swollen from me pinching and biting them and my hand print on your ass from spanking you."

Her eyes widened, and her lips formed a perfect O at his harsh words. But she didn't turn away from him. And she didn't call her dog over to rip out his throat, either.

"So, you're telling me you like to order women around in bed, restrain them, bite them and spank them? This is how you control them?" Disbelief crept into Britt's voice.

"That's part of it, though not as harsh and bleak as you make it sound. At least that's not the way I see it. Let me tell you a little more of my story. Will you listen to me?"

When she nodded, Rick let himself drift back almost thirty years.

"I married Elizabeth right out of college, right after Basic Training, before I went to Officer's School. We had been dating for two years. She had a bachelor's degree in Nursing and I had a degree in International Politics and Geography and a ton of school loans. At that time, my options were limited. I didn't want to teach, and I wasn't sure I wanted law school. So, I looked into the military as a way to pay off my school loans and decided to enlist in the Marines. Elizabeth was fine with my decision. I finished Basic and it turned out, that while I was a helluva marksman, I also had an ear for languages. I was sent for advanced training in Maryland. I was there for two years learning Mandarin, Korean, Arabic, Hebrew, to go with the French and Spanish I took in high school and college. Life was pretty good. I was a second lieutenant, Elizabeth was a nurse at the National Institute of Health, working on infectious diseases. We were happy. Our love life was great: sweet, satisfying, fun—just not too adventurous because, hey, what did we know?" His voice dropped to a harsh whisper.

"We had a kid, right before I got my first deployment. We named him John for my grandfather. I didn't see him or my wife for over a year. When I returned from Africa, he didn't know who I was. I was just making some headway then I was shipped out again. I was gone a long time. By the time I got back Stateside, my marriage was over. She couldn't take the separations. I gave her the divorce with no arguments; she had not signed up for that gig—raising a kid alone for a year at a time. They moved to California. She remarried a few years later, some heart surgeon in San Diego."

Britt just sat watching him, her eyes swimming with tears.

"Anyway, I was travelling all over the world, but mostly in Asia and the Middle East, with some time in Eastern Europe. You know the places I'm talking about. It was too crazy and too dangerous to get involved for any amount of time with any woman. 'Till I met Sybill. She was a State Department attaché. Looked like Mata Hari, if you can believe it and one of the best at the craft of espionage I ever met. We danced around a little bit, then one night after a few too many drinks, we hit the sheets. There was nothing tender about that woman, not a drop of sweet in her. And it worked for me."

Britt hadn't taken her eyes off Rick's face. She seemed mesmerized by his words.

"All the sweet and tender had been leached out of me, too—by what I had seen, what I had done. Elizabeth, she saw it in me, that first time I came back, and it just got worse. Sybill was the same. The only way it worked for her was rough. She needed pain with her pleasure. And I realized that I didn't want anyone who could make me feel what I had felt for Elizabeth; I couldn't let my guard down enough to love like that again. Well, me and Sybby, we got drunk enough on some down time in Vegas to get married. And six weeks later, when we finally sobered up, we got divorced in Mexico. That was it for me. There were other women, to be sure, over the years, but I had to take control. To protect me and to protect them."

Britt was silent, her face was unreadable. She turned to look out at the ocean, as if the answer to their dilemma was going to come riding in on the waves. When she spoke, her voice was as distant as the cold, dry mountains of Afghanistan.

"I understand. What you saw, what I saw, what we had to do to survive in the places we've been, changes a person—man or woman."

When she looked back at him, her lips curved in a small, sad smile, and she laid her hand on his. His hope soared at the simple gesture.

"I was, I mean, I *am* a social worker. I got my degree in Social Work in Indiana and had just completed my MSW at Columbia and gotten my license when 9/11 happened. I was doing community counseling in the Bronx and I thought that I had seen a lot on those mean streets. But, once I enlisted in the Army, I realized that I knew very little about man's inhumanity to man. Before the CST program opened up, I was doing counseling at a base hospital in Texas. A lot of veterans were coming back from Iraq then and, again, I thought I had heard the worst. It wasn't until I was actually in Iraq and Afghanistan, in combat situations, that I had any clue about what those men and women had faced. And even then, I was trained and armed, but I never killed anyone. I questioned some women in Afghanistan, but I never was involved in enhanced interrogation. I didn't have blood on my hands. At least, not until the night Nadia was killed."

When Rick started to protest that it hadn't been her fault, she held up her hand. "Let me finish. But after that night, after all those months in hospitals, away from my unit, away from Alex, I had withdrawn so far into myself, I didn't know if I would ever feel anything again. So, I kind of get what you are saying. "But," and she leaned toward him, both her hands taking his, "I felt everything last night when you were inside me. I felt the excitement, the heat, the care you took with me. I'm not in love with you, but I felt affection, lust. And trust. And I didn't need to be in control."

She let go of his hands and looked him straight in the eye. Tears were streaming down her face. "I don't know if I can cede the kind of control you believe you need to be able to be with me. I don't know if I want to. I have to think. Alone."

Rick left without saying a word. Back on his own deck, he glanced over at Britt's cottage. Her deck was empty of woman and dog. Just his bottle of gin was left, the late afternoon sun glinting off its blue surface.

He went inside and climbed the stairs to his office space. As long as he was going to be alone, waiting for her decision, he was going to do some digging. "I made her cry, god damn it. At least I can find the guy who almost got her killed. And then he'll be doing more than crying."

CHAPTER SEVENTEEN

I t had been a long day. Britt leaned against the deck railing, watching the dark waves break on the shore, the foam billows of white in the moonlight. It was her favorite time of day at the beach. No one was about, lights in houses up and down the coast had flickered on. The sound of the ocean and the night breeze drowned out everything else. She felt peaceful and protected, alone in the pretty cottage, her faithful dog sleeping on the couch. They'd had a long walk after dinner, a solitary meal Britt ate while standing in her kitchen, her eyes deliberately looking away from Rick's beach house.

She turned her head to see if he was anywhere around. The light over the door onto the deck cast a soft glow over empty chairs. Another light shone from an upstairs window. She had seen no sign of her one-time lover since he had left her that afternoon. Glancing back through her deck doors, Britt smiled at the sight of Alex sprawled across the deep blue sofa. He would be out for several hours, she knew, after a day of sun, beach, two meals, and several snacks.

A light went on in Rick's kitchen. Britt took a deep breath as her heart began to hammer. "Well, there's no time like the present." She straightened up, reached for the bottle of gin that had been left on the deck table and made her way down to the beach. It was only twenty-five steps to Rick's staircase, but she dragged her bare feet through the sand, counting each one off. Within minutes she was standing outside his door. Through the gauzy curtains, she could see him standing in front of the open refrigerator door. Before her nerves could defeat her, she rapped once on the door. His head whipped around, a look of surprise and annoyance on his face. She smirked. "Ha, ha. Lost in thought, Marine, and you're pissed you didn't hear me approaching. Score one for me."

Consternation had been replaced on his face with pleasant neutrality by the time he opened the door.

"Hello, would you like to come in?"

"Yes, thank you. I saw you left your gin on my table, so I thought I would bring it over." That was the lie she had rehearsed as she dressed earlier in slim white slacks and a loose black top. Her hair was down, and large silver hoop earrings were her only jewelry.

His raised eyebrow as he stepped aside for her to enter told her that he recognized her greeting for the lie it was. "God, he really is a damn sexy man," she thought, her gaze taking in the black T-shirt that showcased his broad chest and narrow waist. The faded and torn blue jeans were a soft caress down his long legs and around his very fine ass. They stood facing each other. Britt knew he was waiting for her to continue so she squared her shoulders and let him have it.

"I've been thinking about what you said, and I've decided to try it your way."

His stunned expression would have made her laugh except she had seen the momentary flare of victory in his eyes. She felt like she was going into battle again, but on an unknown battleground against a far more experienced opponent.

Rick didn't move. "I'm not sure what you mean."

"You're not easy, Marine, are you? You want me to spell it out? Okay. I want to have sex with you, here, tonight, with you in control. I believe that is how you described your preferences. I'll do what you tell me to do." She could see desire on his face, his lips parting on a long sigh. "But, I draw the line on spanking, I don't want that, and I don't see how it could possibly make me want you." She paused and licked her lips. "Any more than I already want you."

He still hadn't moved. Damn, he was good at this cat and mouse game. "What made you change your mind?"

"Many things. I'll tell you about most of them after. But, I just thought that I had said no to you earlier without really understanding what exactly you wanted and without considering whether I might enjoy some of the things you mentioned." She could feel her cheeks getting warm as she thought about what he had described.

He saw it, too, she realized, when he replied, in that low, husky whisper that made her insides melt. "So, you want to see what it's like when I bite your nipples while I hold your hands behind your back?"

Her traitorous nipples hardened into diamond-sharp peaks at his words. She licked her lips again and was pleased to see the way his eyes fastened on her mouth and the bulge that had appeared under his fly. "Yes. Do you?"

Rick closed the few steps between them in an instant. His mouth was on hers, his tongue buried in its depths. Britt raised her hands toward his shoulders to steady herself, but he clasped them in his hands and drew her arms behind her back. He had a firm grip on her wrists before he lowered his mouth to her breasts. She could feel his hot breath on her nipples and her back arched to bring her closer to his mouth. He flicked his tongue over one nipple, making her gasp. But when his teeth closed over her she let out a faint scream. He didn't stop, biting gently then with increasing pressure until she thought she was going to come standing there, fully clothed, in his living room.

His free hand pushed under her loose top and pulled her bra down, freeing her breast. His tongue licked away the sting from his bites, laving her nipple with long slow licks. He looked up at her grinning, "Nice bra, Blondie. I love black lace."

She gasped. "Wait 'til you see the thong."

That seemed to be all the incentive he needed. She was swept up in his powerful arms and before she could utter a word, he was carrying her upstairs. Rick plopped her down on his huge bed and came down

next to her. His mouth was fastened on her breast while his hands worked to free her from her bra and blouse. Soon she was naked from the waist up, twisting under the twin attacks from his mouth and his hands, trying to touch him anywhere.

"No. No touching," he almost barked at her. "Hands above your head."

As she complied, he reached into her waistband and pulled her slacks off and tossed them on the floor. Britt lay there clad only in a black and white polka dot thong, another of Aunt Susan's purchases. She felt an embarrassed flush creeping up her torso to her cheeks. Wanting desperately to cover herself with her hands, she nonetheless obeyed his command and kept her hands clasped over her head.

Rick sat back on his heels and let his eyes play over her. She knew he was assessing every scar, analyzing how old it was, and what weapon had caused the disfiguring mark. Then he leaned down and kissed her belly. His tongue trailed down to her navel. It was so sweet a gesture that she felt a tear trickle down her cheek, but she made no move to wipe it away.

"God, you're gorgeous. Tough and tender. That is certainly you, Captain." Rick threw her a jaunty mock salute before he pulled his T-shirt over his head revealing a torso also marked with scars. Before she could make a comment that he looked all tough and not tender, he lifted her knee to his lips and traced the long angry red line with his tongue. He didn't stop mid-thigh when he encountered unmarked skin, his mouth drifted higher and higher leaving a wet trail all the way to the polka dots covering her pussy. His long clever fingers slid easily past her panties and into her silky depths. He curled them into her, zeroing in on her most sensitive spot as if he had radar on his fingertips.

Britt was desperate to touch her clever lover. Her hands were starting to slide out from under her head when he reached up and pinned them to the bed with one strong hand, his other never stopping the strokes that were about to send her screaming into climax.

"Come for me, Britt. Come for me. Now." And his fingers plunged deep within her. Her ass came off the bed in a quick jerk, then collapsed as wave after wave of pleasure flowed through her. When her eyes fluttered open a moment later, Rick was kneeling over her, with a very satisfied grin on his face. He bent to kiss her, a quick nip on her lower lip. God, he was right, she thought, as she felt an answering tremor deep within her. Pain with pleasure. His mouth drifted across her chin and down her neck. Then, his tongue was tracing the cluster of shrapnel scars that ran from her collarbone to her shoulder. She started to pull away, embarrassed to have him that close to the puckered tissue. He pushed her back down on the bed.

"I told you not to move, soldier. And I mean it. You're not going to get away with trying to hide battle scars from me. They almost cost you your life and to me, they're a beautiful reminder of what you survived." He sat back up, pointing to the long scar that ran from his back, and down his side to his navel. "Knife, Somalia." He twisted so she could see the cluster of circular scars on his back. "Bullets, Bosnia." His fingers touched a small scar above his eyebrow. "Hand to hand, Iraq. There are a few others hidden in my hair and an embarrassing one on my ass that was no one's fault by my own. So, don't ever cover up for me, Britt. It pisses me off."

Before she could find her voice, in a throat clogged with emotion, he had moved down her body again, taking her panties with him. He stood at the end of the bed, and quickly removed his jeans.

"Commando, of course," Britt thought, her mouth watering at the sight of his throbbing erection.

He knelt between her legs, sliding his hands up their long lean length, until he was cupping her ass. She was completely open to him.

Lifting her tush off the bed, Rick slid her up on his thigh until his cock was pressing into the wet folds at her center. "Put your legs up on my shoulders, darlin', and cross your ankles. It's going to be a rough ride." As she was complying with his directive, his long hard cock slid into her. His hands tilted her ass up a little more and he was buried in her. The he began to move, all the way out, then all the way in, the speed and force increasing with each thrust. Her hands gripped the comforter behind her head and her shins were pressed against his neck. Britt was totally possessed by her fierce warrior; he was quickly breaching her defenses. Her pussy was tightening and tried to push back against him, but his hands anchored her in place. Tightening her vaginal muscles held him briefly but then his thrusts increased in speed and force until she was screaming her release. His continued movements were almost too much to bear and she was about to beg him to stop, that she couldn't take another orgasm, when he tightened within her and the violent pulses of his release filled her.

Collapsing on the bed, Rick pulled Britt into his arms. They were both breathing like they'd run up the side of a mountain in full battle gear. Britt lay motionless, not sure whether she was permitted to hold or touch Rick. His hands were stroking her back and her ass as his breathing returned to normal.

"Are you okay?" he asked quietly.

Her head pressed against his chest. She barely nodded, still unable to speak, overwhelmed by the intensity of his love-making. "Yes," was almost just a sigh escaping from her swollen lips. They rested there for a few moments before Britt spoke. "I need to use the bathroom."

Rick immediately released her and pointed to the door across from the bed. "Just through there, darlin'."

Her reflection in the mirror startled Britt. Her hair was a tangled mass, her lips were red and swollen and there was a slight bruise on her breast. She looked well and truly fucked. She grinned. After washing up, she looked around for a towel or robe to wrap herself in but remembering Rick's admonition that he never wanted to see her covering up her scars, with a toss of her head, she threw her hair back and marched into the bedroom.

Rick was sitting on the edge of the bed, as naked as she was. His smile broadened as he stood. "My turn, darlin'. And, Captain," he said as he strode past her, "high marks for that in-your-face entrance."

She stuck her tongue out at him when she heard the door close. By the time he returned, she was fully dressed, standing in the doorway out to the deck, watching the ocean. Rick came up behind her, his hands on her shoulders.

"So, I take it you're not going to stay?"

"No, thank you, I can't. Alex is okay for a few hours alone at night, but he'll be up soon for his just-before-midnight-pee and I have to be there to let him out." She turned to him. "Why don't you put some clothes on and walk over with me. There's something I'd like to show you."

His eyes widened. "Yes, ma'am. Just let me get dressed and I'll follow you anywhere."

CHAPTER EIGHTEEN

Rick was right behind her. She knew he was probably thinking that he was going to get lucky again. Britt smiled to herself as she bent to pet Alex's big furry head. Well, he probably would be having sex with her again in the next few hours. If he could accept her truths.

There was a light tap on the deck doors. Rick was waiting to be invited in, the soft glow from the outdoor light spilling over him like a silver mantle. A knight in slightly tarnished armor, she thought, as she stepped over to open the door.

"How's your trusty watchdog?"

"Dead to the world. We had quite a long walk on the beach earlier. I was feeling like I had been neglecting him. And I needed the exercise, too."

Rick smiled at her as he, too, reached down to stroke Alex's soft yellow fur. "You're so good with him. He's lucky to have you."

"I'm lucky to have *him*. I love him more than any other creature in the world. There's only one other who has come close to him in taking over my heart." Rick looked startled. She held out her hand to him. "Come with me."

He took her outstretched hand, giving it a gentle squeeze before he pulled her over to plant a light kiss on her cheek. "Thank you for earlier. It meant a lot to me that you decided to give my way a chance, darlin'. To try to trust me."

She returned the squeeze to his hand, as she pulled him toward her bedroom. "It seemed the right thing to do. It took me some time today to work it out. A few months ago, I wouldn't have been able to kiss you, much less trust you to make love to me in *any* way. And most certainly not with you taking away my control."

In her bedroom, Britt let go of his hand, leaving him standing in the middle of the room. She reached for a framed photograph, partially hidden behind a stack of books on her dresser. Climbing up onto her bed, she sat against the headboard and patted the spot next to her. "Come sit beside me, Marine, I've got a story to tell you."

Rick laid down on his stomach next to her, his eyes full of questions. She handed him the photograph. It was a picture of an even-thinner Britt, her arms wrapped around a gorgeous golden horse. Her face was a vision of love. The horse was leaning his head against her, a look of complete devotion in his eyes.

"This is Kip. His racing name is Groom's Point. He's a retired thoroughbred race horse and he saved my life." She paused to wipe a tear from her eyes.

"When I was in the hospitals in Germany and Washington, I was a mess. I mean, physically, I was being taken care of—I had the best surgeons, all the physical therapy I needed and more than I wanted. But emotionally, I was just retreating into myself. I couldn't seem to wrap my head around what had happened in Afghanistan, how badly I was injured, how Nadia died on my watch. I could barely speak, and I was useless in the counseling sessions. I started having nightmares. I was given psych medicine, but I was afraid to take it. I didn't see the point in even trying. But, my physical injuries were healed, and they had to discharge me. Physically, I looked like I was on the road to recovery. I had pretty much full range of motion in my knee, the shrapnel wounds to my shoulder had healed, and I had no apparent damage from the concussion. But, inside my head, I was a train wreck."

Rick was nodding his head. "I know what you mean. I've seen it before, dozens of times in the past twenty years."

Britt stared at him, smiling softly. She wondered if he had any clue that he was one of the walking wounded, that he had been as damaged emotionally as she had been—probably worse. But she held her tongue, deciding to tell him her story and gauge his reaction before she started chipping away at the wall he had built around his heart.

"Well, I wasn't sure where I wanted to go. I'd sublet an apartment in Texas, near the base where I'd been assigned before I deployed. It had become more a storage unit for the stuff I'd accumulated over the years than it was a home. But I landed back in Texas, with scrips for PT appointments for follow-up and a referral for mental health therapy, if I wanted it. I didn't want *any* of it. I was tired of feeling like a stranger had climbed inside my skin. I didn't recognize my own face in the mirror half the time. And I had no idea how to deal with the person who was inhabiting my body."

She ran her hands down her legs, left them resting palm-up on her knees. Rick reached over to take one of her hands in his own. He raised it to his lips for a sweet kiss.

"There was a bar near my apartment complex, a hangout for Army veterans, and I started spending some time there. No, I was spending a *lot* of time there. Some of the vets were way older than me, like from Vietnam, and some had just come back from Iraq or Afghanistan. Mostly guys, but a few women hung there, too. I was slipping further and further away from everyday living, from being able to get up in the morning or sleep at night. Anyway, I'm sitting there one night, nursing a Jameson on the rocks, and this good ole boy slides into a seat two bar stools away from me. He looked familiar, I'd seen him in there several times since I'd started hanging out in that bar. He glances over at me, nods his head, takes a sip of beer and just starts talking. I'm trying to ignore him. But he just keeps talking about how rough it was when he got home, how he was making a mess of his marriage, fucking up on the job. The whole PTSD screwed up vet story, you know? Then his face kind of lights up when he tells me about this program that matches veterans with retired thoroughbred race horses. It's called Saratoga War Horse and its free for vets to participate. He slides this card over to me and says, 'your face looks like mine did when I got home from Iraq. This program saved my life. All you have to do is take the first step. Make the call.' Then, he up and leaves. It took me a few days and a few more sleepless nights before I dialed the number on the card.''

There were tears in her eyes. Rick sat up and held her for a while, just rubbing her back, nothing more. Britt breathed in deeply, raggedly, and gave him a tremulous smile. "This is the first time I've really talked about this with anyone."

"You're such a brave girl, darlin'. You can tell me as much or as little as you want." Hearing this, Britt moved out of his arms and twisted around to sit, facing him.

"I saved the card, then I threw it away. I was not brave, I was scared. Then I fished the card out of the wastebasket. It took me a week to get up the nerve to call the number that veteran had given me. The wisest decision I ever made." She sighed, then straightened her shoulders like the soldier she still was and continued in a voice filled with wonder.

"When I called, I spoke with a guy who had flown Medevac helicopters in Vietnam. I told him about the vet who gave me his card. He didn't seem surprised. We talked for a long time and when I spoke about my depression and nightmares, he invited me to fly up to New York and check out the program. I was skeptical, and he didn't pressure me but there was an opening in the program starting the next month, so I had to decide. So, I went. No charge, they covered the flight, my room in a hotel in Saratoga where the other participants were staying, all our meals, transportation to the farm, everything. Not all the vets were from Iraq or Afghanistan. One had fought in Vietnam, one had been in Bosnia, others in Desert Storm—just about every war, conflict and shit storm where our armed forces have served. We had dinner together with the staff and talked about the program and our own history. The next morning, we were at the farm to meet with the Equine Director about what to expect. That afternoon we each went into the ring separately with the Equine Director.

She matched each of us with a horse. I got Kip. God, he was beautiful. He reminded me of Alex with his golden mane. So, my turn came, and I went into the ring with him, just the two of us and that's when the miracle happened. It was like a switch had been turned on inside me."

She smiled. "My nervous system was reset. Can you imagine? By learning to communicate with a horse, a flight creature, my autonomic nervous system was re-regulated. I'm a social worker, I've done therapy for years with soldiers, with people who had suffered trauma. But, I can't truly explain what happened to me in that ring when Kit came to me, when his eyes met mine and he leaned his face against my shoulder. I had my arms around him in an instant, crying like a baby."

The tears that had gathered in her eyes spilled over, cascading down her cheeks. Britt wiped her nose on her sleeve. "God, I'm such a mess. Look at me, blubbering like a baby."

Rick handed her a box of Kleenex from the bedside table. He sat, facing her, his eyes deep blue with admiration, while she wiped tears from her face and cleaned up her runny nose. He reached out for her, gently, almost hesitantly. "I need to kiss you, *Wonder Woman*. Are you okay with that? Let me kiss you, now. Please."

"No." His eyes opened wider in surprise at her succinct and immediate denial of his request. Disappointment was evident on his handsome face. Laughing, Britt pushed Rick onto his back and slid up his body, cradling his face in her hands, before she lowered her mouth to his.

CHAPTER NINETEEN

Some kisses stay with you for the rest of your life. Sometimes it's your first kiss, sometimes it's the kiss from a special occasion and sometimes it's a kiss that comes at you from left field and changes your life forever. All Rick could think, and he was not thinking very clearly, was a fragment of a line from one of his favorite movies: that since the first kiss ever only a very few had been rated as passionate and pure, but none as perfect as this kiss. He knew as Britt's warm, wet mouth caressed his lips that on his dying day, if her kiss was the last sweet memory he had, he would die a contented man. He fought the need to reach up and cover her hands with his own and pull them down to her sides.

Her slight weight was like a warm blanket covering him. Her soft full breasts cushioned against his chest and he could feel the sharp points of her hip bones poking into his belly. Strong yet frail, courageous yet frightened, Britt was devouring him and destroying him. When her sweet tongue plunged between his lips and swept along his teeth, Rick surrendered to her conquest. His hands crept up from the bed to lightly caress her hips, but he made no other move.

Britt's weight shifted as she straightened up into a sitting position on his throbbing erection, her legs straddling him, bent at the knees.

Her hands captured his hands and brought them around to where she clasped them on his chest. Long silver and gold hair framed her face like some unearthly lion's mane.

"You're mine now, Marine. For me to do with as I please."

"Yes, ma'am." A slow grin spread across Rick's face. "Whatever you want."

"I want you to watch." Britt shifted slightly again, and the movement of her heated center rocking against his aching cock almost made him come. Pulling her shirt over her head, she tossed it on the floor next to her bed, where it fell with a silky sigh. Her hands cupped her full breasts, confined within the black lace cups of her bra. He watched dry-mouthed as her thumbs swept back and forth over her nipples, tightening them into stiff peaks.

He started to unclench his hands to reach up and unhook the front clasp on her bra but a stern look from Britt had Rick folding his hands again on his chest. His eyes widened with desire when she did for herself what he longed to do, freeing her breasts from their lacy barriers. Her bra joined her blouse on the floor. God, he wanted to touch her, but he didn't want to break the spell she was weaving with her bold and sexy moves. As if sensing his thoughts, Britt covered her breasts with Rick's hands, her breath catching as his fingers closed around her and his thumbs pressed against her nipples.

Then, she leaned into his hands, encouraging him to squeeze her breasts. He lifted his head from the bed and licked her nipples as they poked between his fingers.

"Mmmm, oh yeah. Yes."

Rick increased the pressure of his mouth on her. And before she could tell him anything else, his teeth delicately took her nipples between them.

She didn't pull away. Instead, she reached between them and began unfastening the button on his jeans, trying to slide her fingers into the waistband.

It was killing him not to roll her over and plunge inside her, but Rick was determined to let Britt lead the way, to see if he could surrender to her control. He moaned against her breasts, as his hands drifted down to her hips.

After pulling his jeans off and tossing them on the floor, she slid farther down on his torso to give herself access to his cock. Her breasts popped out of his mouth. He let his head fall back on the bed, admiring how her nipples glistened like rubies in the cool evening air of the bedroom. His admiration was short-lived because his eyes crossed when he felt the exotic bloom that was her mouth close around the swollen tip of his erection. She was sliding down between his legs, her mouth still fastened on his penis. Little flickers of fire engulfed him every time she licked or nipped. Once again, he strained to control the urge to clasp her head in his hand and push his cock all the way down her throat. Instead, he let the passion build as she licked, sucked, and bit until he was throbbing with need.

"Darlin', whatever you want is fine with me, but if you don't stop I'm going to come in that clever mouth of yours. You've got about five seconds to decide."

Britt looked up with an amused smile on her face, her eyes large dark pools of indigo in the faint light of the bedroom. But she rose again and rolled onto her back. Shimmying, raising her ass up from the bed, she quickly pulled off her slim slacks and panties, and rolled back onto him. Rising up above him, she slowly seated herself in his lap, his cock sliding deep within her.

With their eyes locked, their hands clasped together and resting on her knees, she rode him like an Olympic equestrienne, like a cowgirl in heat. The pressure built fast in him; he couldn't believe how much he wanted her for their second time that night. Soon the air was thick with the smell of sweat and sex, the slight breeze from the ocean only adding to the humidity that was causing her skin to glisten and beads of sweat to trickle down his neck.

Gasping and crying out his name, Britt bent forward as her orgasm swept through her. She never let go of his hands, even when he pounded up and into her, his own release exploding into her clenching passage.

Finally, when she collapsed on top of him, both of them sucking in air, he wrapped his arms around her. Sleep found them both within minutes, Rick still buried inside Britt.

It seemed like hours later, but it was only a short time, when Rick was awakened by a nudge against his side. Thinking it was Britt trying to get him to move away from her, he managed to prop open an eye. It wasn't Britt. She had obviously slid off him after they fell into sleep and was curled on her side, head on his shoulder, one leg draped over his thigh.

Rick turned his head to the other direction and came face to face with the annoyed brown eyes of a large yellow dog. Alex.

"Okay, buddy," he whispered, "let me just slide out of here and find my jeans." Alex trotted over to the doorway. Rick made quick but silent work out of disentangling himself from Britt and getting out of bed. He grabbed his pants from the floor and stepped into them. Straightening, he paused to gaze at his sleeping lover. She was curled up on her side, silver hair spread across the sheets, looking like an angel, pausing between earth and heaven. "Just a minute, Alex, we don't want her to get cold." He untangled the light comforter from the foot of the bed and drew it up and over her long legs and sweet breasts. A small yip from the direction of the living room made him realize he had just been standing there staring at Britt. *Man, I am toast. I'm practically drooling.*

Alex was waiting by the door for him. The two went out on the deck and Alex dashed down the stairs and off to the side. A few minutes later, he was back by Rick's side. "Is this your midnight run that Britt told me about? Now, you're good for the rest of the night? I hope so. Your mama could use some rest." Rick yawned loudly. "And so could I."

Back inside, Rick tossed the eager Lab a treat and added fresh water to his bowl. Alex trotted back into the bedroom. Rick paused in the living room, looking from the bedroom door to the back door. "Stay or go?" She hadn't asked him to stay, but she'd fallen fast asleep as soon as she had finished with him. Rick's grin split his face. Damn, the woman was something else. Brave enough to try his way and let him take control. And then share a deep dark truth about herself and totally turn him around.

Rick didn't want to leave. He didn't want her to wake up to an empty bed and think it was a "wham, bam, thank you ma'am" deal with him. That last thought had him laughing to himself when he stepped back into Britt's bedroom and found Alex stretched out on one side of the bed, his head resting on her torso. The big dog looked up as if assessing the situation. He cast a questioning eye at Rick and then lifted his head and did a nod and point to Britt's other side.

"Well, I've got the other guy's permission, I might as well stay." He thought this was one of the more bizarre situations in which he had found himself as he stripped off his shorts and climbed into bed. Pulling a bit of the comforter over himself, he settled down next to Britt. Her soft sleeping sounds drifted on the night air, calming him. Rick rested his arm on Britt's hip then reached out a hand to pet Alex's soft fur. *Tonight, at least, all's right with the world.* Then he drifted off to sleep.

CHAPTER TWENTY

The next few days were some of the happiest Rick could remember. Nights filled with dreamless sleep after days on the beach with a crazy dog and a bright and beautiful woman were erasing lines of tension from his face. Lines that had been carved there by sleepless nights and days full of danger, dishonor, and death. Most of his focus was on Britt and Alex and his hardest decisions were whether to cook out or order in, and whether they were sleeping at her house or at his. Alex had come to accept him as a comrade-in-arms and wandered back and forth between the two cottages as if they were both home. Britt, too, was relaxing and becoming comfortable with just running up the steps to his deck and popping in through the usually open doors, calling his name out if she didn't see him in the kitchen or living area.

Sitting upstairs in his office off the guest room, he let out a sigh of relief. She'd come dashing up the stairs just yesterday, calling his name, and he'd barely had time to shut down his laptop before she was leaning over him, her arms wrapped around his neck. She could have seen every damning detail that was displayed on the Department of the Army file he had just managed to hack into.

At least this morning, he had no such worries. Britt had headed off

Long Beach Island early to get to a couple of appointments at a nearby VA hospital. Knee and shoulder assessments, she told him, no big deal —but she wouldn't be back until the afternoon. As a result, he and Alex were hanging out at his cottage, Alex having taken position on the deck outside Rick's bedroom, half in and half out of the shade. Rick realized he liked having a canine companion to run with and relax with, and handily clean up any food that dropped off the table or kitchen island.

Glancing at his watch, he saw that it was approaching noon. He made a quick call to Mick. "Hey, man. I'm dog-sitting today. How about you pick up some sandwiches and come over for lunch on the deck with me and Alex?"

"Jesus, I wish I had a recording device on this phone. I know a dozen guys who would pay good money to hear you invite me for a lunch date with you and your dog!" Mick was laughing. "Where's *Wonder Woman* today?"

"Britt's at the VA getting her knee and shoulder looked at and picking up some meds. She won't be back 'til later this afternoon."

"Oh, and you're so hooked on her that you can't stand to be alone for a few hours? This is priceless coming from the man who once holed up in a cave for seventeen days with no radio and only a camel for companionship."

"No. Well, yes. I'm getting hooked, I guess. But, I'm craving an Italian mix and some potato salad—I have beer—and I need to talk to you."

"I'm a little rusty on dating advice, bro, so I don't know how much help I'm going to be. But, I do know where the best Italian mixed can be found so I guess I'm your guy. I'll see you in thirty minutes."

Mick arrived on time. "Damn, the man is never late," Rick remembered. If they were to rendezvous at 0900 hours, Mick's tanks would be idling at the designated location at precisely 0900. Made Rick crazy and eternally grateful to his fellow Marine who had helped him save countless missions. And lives.

After dropping two large brown bags on the deck table, Mick flopped into the chair and reached for the frosty beer bottle waiting for him. Alex was sitting by Rick's side, eyeing the new arrival with some suspicion and a great deal of interest in the smells from the bags Mick had delivered. Mick held out his hand for Alex to sniff. "That is one good-looking dog you've got, bro."

"Yes, he's a good boy. Alex, this is Mick. He's okay, he's a friend. It's okay." With Rick's words, Alex moved over to Mick's side, licked his hand then placed a paw on the big man's knee. That brought a laugh from both men.

"We had Labs growing up, they're the best dogs. My mom always said they were opportunistic feeders. Is it okay if he has part of my sandwich? I've got roast beef." Mick was already reaching into the bag.

"Yeah, Britt lets him have beef and turkey, no salami or ham. He'll love you forever for a little roast beef. And cheese. The damn dog loves cheese. Especially American cheese." Rick shook his head at the Lab's enthusiastic appetite.

"Well, he's an Army dog, after all. Right? Red, white and blue."

"Actually, he was a stray, digging around in the garbage outside the base in Kandahar. An officer found him and brought him into the unit. He kind of became one of their mascots. From what I understand, he was getting pretty good at sniffing out strange packages or concealed contraband. He didn't go on missions, but he was sort of assigned to the clinic where Britt and some nurses and therapists were working with the civilian women. He found a few weapons underneath all those robes and wraps."

Mick was digging into his sandwich, pulling out shredded roast beef and dropping it on the deck for Alex. Except, it never reached the deck, Alex easily caught the offerings mid-air. Mick looked up at Rick, an accusatory gleam in his eye. "Wait a minute. You didn't get all that from Britt. That sounds like it came straight from a unit report." He put his sandwich back down on the deli wrap on the table. "You've been digging. You know who the guy is."

Rick threw him a smart salute then took a long draw on his beer. "Damn straight I do. Lieutenant Colonel Jonathan "Jake" Gable. Currently assigned to DOD, but formerly a Battalion Commander in Afghanistan. At Kandahar. Took command of a mission seeking to bring down a notorious war lord with close ties to the Taliban and maybe Al Qaeda, thought to be hiding out at an armed compound about an hour from Kandahar. Mission got fucked up. One civilian and one Army interpreter dead. One Captain seriously injured. All women. Said Lieutenant Colonel quietly transferred from his command to a desk job in DC after several months of 'unofficial' investigations. Like I said when Britt told me her version of the story: bullshit."

"Damn. Damn. I'm not even going to ask you how you got this information. I really don't need to ask you, I know. But, damn." Mick took a long drink from his beer. "What are you going to do now? I know the answer but tell me anyway. This is going to be a fucking cluster-fuck."

"That's why I called you over here. A month ago, if I found out shit like this, I'd be making calls and looking for heads to roll. But, now, with Britt, I'm not sure. I don't know how much she knows. I'm certain it's more than she told me, but I can't prove it. And she's come so far, I don't want to cause any setbacks. But, I fucking want to strangle this guy, hang him by his thumbs from a cliff over shark-infested waters, cut his balls off, bust him to private...you name it."

"Yeah, but you getting thirty years in Leavenworth solves nothing and would just piss me off. Who would save me from the dietary hell my daughters have consigned me to?" The two men sat and silently stared out at the Atlantic for several moments. Rick broke the silence.

"Well, I'm going to pass this information on to some of our old friends. I can't stand the notion that this scumbag is still in uniform, that good men and women have to salute this motherfucker. And, I'm not going to tell Britt. Not now, anyway. I didn't have to use her name, access her records, or contact any of her fellow soldiers."

Mick nodded his head in agreement. "Yeah, this asshole has to be gone. Dishonorable discharge if he doesn't resign his commission. Period. No discussion. Not telling Britt? That I'm not sure about. I don't know the lady. I know what she's gone through—some of it, anyway." Mick was rubbing his chest over his heart in a way Rick had seen him do a thousand times. "I don't know how I'd feel if I learned that I was injured because one of my own fucked up. Or even worse, deliberately put me in harm's way. I don't know how that would help me even if I knew he or she'd been punished. It wouldn't give me back my heart, my finger, or all the years in uniform I lost. Especially, since being shot gave me so many years with Annie that I would never have been able to recapture if I'd retired after twenty years instead of taking a medical discharge."

"Part of me wishes I had taken your advice and not dug into this. I don't want to hurt Britt. Man, I'm really starting to…I don't know…I just think she's amazing. And I'm sleeping through the night." Rick was shaking his head in disbelief.

Mick almost spit out his sip of beer. "Jesus, you're a piece of work. You've got this fantastic woman and the best you can say about your relationship is that you're sleeping good? Damn, bro. You are in worse shape than I thought." But, then he smiled at his old friend. "Actually, that's probably one of the highest compliments you could give her. And I think she'd like it. A lot. Good for you."

Their companionable laughter filled the air, waking up Alex, who joined in with a few playful barks. The three warriors sat on the deck, basking in the sun, the cool breeze and each other's company. Grateful to be home and to have each other. Worried thoughts about what was to come intervened and clouded the afternoon for only one of them.

CHAPTER TWENTY-ONE

"Hey, honey, you home?" Carole Capshaw Ruggiero's voice rang out across the deck. Britt hurried from the bedroom, across the living room and into her aunt's arms.

"It's so good to see you! I didn't expect you for another hour!" Britt hugged her favorite, and only, aunt and her closest relative.

"Your uncle only let me stop once on the Turnpike to pee. So, excuse me, but I have to go. He's right behind me, loaded with bags. I did a little shopping on our drive up from Florida." Her aunt exited the living room in a hurry, heading to the guest bathroom.

Bill Ruggiero, sweating and cursing under his breath, was crossing the deck, laden with several bags of various sizes. Alex was joyfully dancing around his legs. "Alex! Calm it down, boy. If you trip me, we're both going to be sorry. Too bad Britt hasn't trained you to be a pack animal, I'd send you back for the luggage." He looked up and saw Britt in the doorway. "Honey, grab two of these bags before I drop them. Your aunt will kill me. God, the woman can shop!'

Brit divested her uncle of two huge bags stuffed with what looked like towels and placed them on the sofa. Her uncle had just dropped his armful of shopping bags on the dining table. "Come here and let me look at you, sweetheart. Oh, my, you are looking so much better than last month. I knew the Shore was what you needed."

Tears pricked her eyes as the big man, gentle as a teddy bear, wrapped her in his arms. He planted a kiss on her forehead and gave her a squeeze. "You look good, Britt. Healthy," and, drawing away from her, his eyes searching her face, "and happy, too. It must be Alex. You finally have your doggie boy with you. I knew he would put the twinkle back in your eyes."

Britt blushed at her uncle's words. Bill Ruggiero was a genial giant of a man with a huge laugh. But his jovial demeanor hid a discerning eye and a mind like a steel trap. There was not much that got by Uncle Bill. He'd been Army too, serving in Vietnam, before he came home and joined his family's successful construction company. Since 1978, he'd been married to Carole, Britt's mother's only sibling. Their two sons ran the company now, though Bill was still CEO.

"Yes, Uncle Bill, it's great to have Alex. He gets me up every morning, even when I hide under the covers to get a few more minutes of sleep. I can't thank you enough for all you did to get him Stateside. And for the cottage here. The beach is wonderful. I love it." She had tears in her eyes.

"Oh, honey, it was no problem. Of course, we'd do anything we could for you. Especially help rescue a handsome, heroic fellow like Alex from the wilds of Afghanistan. And, this place is yours for as long as you need it. Your aunt has been getting some serious retail therapy in Florida. I don't think she misses the Shore at all."

Laughter was heard from the hallway as Carole came into the room. "Well, I am loving all the outlet malls and flea markets in Florida. Such great deals to be had! They practically give the stuff away." She stuck her tongue out at the knowing looks on their faces. "Besides, it's not like we don't have a beach right outside our house in Clearwater. And the Yankees right across the bay." Aunt Carole had become a die-hard Yankees fan when she had moved from Ohio to New Jersey after marrying Bill. "Here, let me show you what I bought."

Bill backed away from the shopping show and tell. "I'll just go down to the car and get our bags. I'll use the stairs down to the garage." He moved over to the door downstairs and disappeared.

Carole shook her finger at Britt. "Mark my words, he'll sneak down to the corner bar and grab a beer, so he can watch some sports channel. The man has become a golf fanatic. He plays every day."

"I should go down and help him. It's too much for him to haul suitcases up those stairs."

Carole stopped her. "I packed one small suitcase for both of us to use while we're here." They were stopping with Britt for a couple of days at most on their way to Boston for the wedding of the daughter of Bill's cousin. "I packed the big suitcase with all that we need for the wedding weekend. He'll just leave that in the car."

She motioned to Britt. "Do you have any iced tea or lemonade? Why don't you get us each a glass of something cold and I'll show you all this stuff I know you will love. Or at least you will pretend to love because your momma, God rest her soul, raised you right." She wiped a tear from her eye. "How are you doing, honey, really? Is it hard being here in New Jersey? I hope it doesn't cause you too many bad memories."

Britt put two tall glasses of lemonade on the coffee table and gave her aunt another hug. "No, Aunt Carole, I'm fine here. It's always been a happy place and, anyway, we only came here a couple of times together. I made my peace with losing mom and dad. I miss them every day but I stopped dwelling on it. You know my mantra now: there's a difference between mourning and suffering."

"Going to Saratoga was one of the best decisions you ever made, my dear. You came back almost like the niece we have always known and loved. And as I look at you now, you seem to be the person you were before you went overseas that last time. Actually, you look better —happier—than you have in years." She patted the sofa. "Sit down and tell me the truth about what—or who—is responsible for that twinkle in your eye."

Britt sank down next to her aunt and took a sip of lemonade. "Well, I met someone."

"Who?" Her aunt interrupted. "Is it anyone we know? Someone local or at the VA hospital? Tell me."

"Well, actually, it's Rick."

"Our next-door neighbor, Rick?" Carole could not hide the disbelief in her voice.

"Yes, he came back right before the Fourth of July. We saw each other from the decks and started talking." She stopped at the look of utter amazement on her aunt's face.

"Oh, honey," her aunt proclaimed. "We better make snacks. I want to hear every word of this story and I think you are going to need some energy to tell it. You and the ever-elusive Rick. I can't believe it!"

CHAPTER TWENTY-TWO

R ick received a text from Bill Ruggiero: *Hey, we're here. Carole is at the cottage with Britt. I'm at the sports bar. Come meet me for a G&T.* Rick responded that he would be there in ten minutes. Glad to see the neighbor who had become his friend, nervous about spending time with Britt's closest male relative.

True to his word, Rick came strolling through the door of the bar in less than the allotted time. Bill rose to clasp his hand and clap him on the back in a traditional manly greeting. In the years that the two men had been neighbors, a genuine friendship, born of respect and shared experiences, had grown between them. They slid into the booth sitting across from each other.

"Hey, old man. I didn't know you were coming back up to the Shore this summer." Rick signaled the bartender that he wanted what Bill was drinking. "What's up?"

"Family wedding in Boston next weekend so the wife figures we can do a shopping tour of the East Coast if we drive. I've been on the road for four days. I can make it from Clearwater to Surf City in less than a day if I want to, but no. I'm meandering from outlet mall to flea market to roadside stands like the end of the world is approaching and, God forbid, we haven't bought everything in the whole damn country." He took a sip of his drink and grinned. "But Carole is as happy as a clam so I'm fine with it. You know what they say: happy wife, happy life."

Rick nodded his thanks as a huge gin and tonic was placed before him. "I can't say that I've had much experience with that concept, but I'll take your word for it."

"Well, how about this one: happy niece, I'm at peace. I just made that up after spending some time with Britt. From the look that just crossed your face, I'm guessing I might have you to thank for that."

Somewhat taken aback that his usual poker face had given him away, Rick had the good grace to shrug off his minor annoyance at Bill's statement. The older man had known him for almost twenty years, known him as well as anyone with the exception of Mick. "Well, we've been spending some time together since I got here late on July third. I thought I'd keep an eye out on her once I saw she was recovering from some serious injuries." At Bill's snort of derision, Rick laughed. "Yeah, well, I learned pretty quickly that she doesn't need or want much help. And, of course, there's that behemoth of a dog to get past, too. But Alex and I have made our peace since we both have the same goal. Britt and I are still finding our way."

Rick paused to assess the impact of his confession on Bill. He did not expect to see tears in the other man's eyes, even though he knew him to be an old softie.

"Thank you, Rick. It makes me very happy to hear that you have taken an interest in Britt. I wondered if you had given up on women, I so rarely have seen you with one or heard you mention any females except your cousins in almost all the time you've been coming to the Shore. And I'm especially glad to see my niece smiling; glowing, really. Poor girl has had a rough time of it, really tragic almost, and I thought that last tour in Afghanistan was going to do her in. She came home about as broken as I've ever seen her, as bad as after 9/11."

"Yes, she told me she'd been living in New York City in 2001 and that she enlisted shortly after the attacks. I guess that the Trade Center debacle had a major impact on her. I know a lot of men and women who joined up after that." Rick stopped when he saw the surprised look on the older man's face.

"The Trade Center? It wasn't the Trade Center planes that ripped the heart out of her, it was Flight 93," Bill paused.

Rick stared at him.

"You don't know? Her parents were on Flight 93. They died in that field in Pennsylvania."

The gin and tonic rose like bile in Rick's throat. How could he have not known? Why didn't Britt tell him her parents had been killed during the 9/11 attacks? Damn, what else hadn't she told him? Then the image of Jake Gable flashed in his mind.

"I didn't know. She didn't say." He tried to keep the hurt from his voice.

"She doesn't talk about it much. It nearly destroyed her. They were the perfect family. Her dad, Steven, was a lawyer. Carole's sister, Judith, was the loan officer at the local credit union. They made a good, solid life for Britt, their only child. They'd been visiting her in Manhattan for a long weekend and then they were flying to San Francisco for a banking conference. It was a working vacation and they hadn't had a vacation in years. Britt showed them around New York. We went up to New York City to see them the day before, took them and Britt out to lunch, then dropped them off at a hotel near Newark airport. They bragged about the good deal they had gotten on the flight from Newark to San Francisco, so they were flying out of there and not Kennedy. They had decided to spend the night near the airport, so they didn't have to get up super early for the flight on September 11. Perfect planning, but you know how that goes. It was such a fucking tragedy that they died. A middle-class, middle aged couple from Ohio, for christsake! What were they doing flying from goddamn New Jersey to San Francisco? They should have stayed home in the Midwest. Driven up to Chicago for a long weekend. Goddamn waste." Bill's face showed the anger and sorrow he felt at the senseless tragedy.

He finished his drink and just sat shaking his head. Rick didn't know what to say to him; he was stunned by the revelation, a little angry and hurt Britt had not seen fit to share this major event in her life with him. It was several minutes before Bill resumed speaking.

"Anyway, it was devastating for Britt. She had no one except for Carole and me and our two boys. And Carole was a basket case at first. She rallied to try to help Britt when she saw how lost the poor girl was, but by then Britt had decided she was joining the battle. Not for revenge like some we knew, but to make sure it never happened again. I tried to talk her out of it; I didn't want her to go to war. Not after what I saw in 'Nam. But she wasn't having any of it. I figured—I hoped—that being female, at least she wouldn't see any action."

It was Rick's turn to snort in derision.

Bill acknowledged the naivete of his assumption with a slight nod of his head. "Yeah, I know, it's a whole new Army, with a whole new set of rules. She started out doing social work after basic, in a hospital in Texas. I was beginning to relax, assuming that was where the Army would leave her because she was doing such a good job. That's when I learned she'd been training and applying for anything that would get her into battle. Then the Army comes up with that CST training—you know about that?" At Rick's short nod, Bill continued. "And off she goes to Afghanistan. I didn't sleep for almost a year. That tour was up, and I thought she'd stay Stateside, but the Army changes the playing field again and back she goes. I'm just grateful that she didn't die in that last attack. Thank God they got her out of there in time to treat her. But, she took the death of her friend, Nadia, really hard. Did she tell you about that?"

"She told me some, I pieced together the rest."

"What rest?" Bill reached out and grabbed hold of Rick's hand. "What rest? Is there something she didn't tell me?"

"There's something I don't think she knows about what happened that night, about why that night went down the way it did. I did some digging and confirmed what I suspected. And I took some steps to make sure the cocksucker responsible for her injuries and her friend's death pays for what he did." Rick was leaning across the table, his voice low and fierce, his eyes cold and deadly.

"Son of a bitch. I'll kill the bastard." Bill's voice rose. He pounded his fist on the table. "Tell me who it was and tell me what you've done."

Both men started at the sound of a cool, too-controlled voice coming from just behind Rick. "Yes, Major, tell us what you've done."

Rick turned to stare into Britt's furious and frozen blue eyes.

CHAPTER TWENTY-THREE

Bill insisted they take their conversation out of the bar and back to the beach house. Britt tromped ahead of the two men, about as angry as she had ever been in her life. Angrier because it was all mixed in with hurt, disappointment, betrayal, and fear. What had Rick done? And what had he told her uncle?

Britt started up the steps to Rick's beach house, freezing when she felt his firm grip on her arm. "Don't touch me, Marine. I can drop-kick you to China from this angle." She snarled the words without turning.

"I think we should go to your place, so your aunt and uncle can hear what I have to say."

Britt turned to face him, then. "My aunt has been through enough, thank you. She doesn't need to get involved with this cluster fuck. This is between you and me."

Steps behind Rick, Bill spoke up. "No, honey, I'm in this too. I want to hear what Rick has to say. And you can use some support, too."

Her shoulders slumped at the steel underlying her uncle's request. She'd have to deal with two men, one she loved better than any man alive and the other? The other, she could have loved even more. "Alright, Uncle Bill. Let's hear what the Marine has to say. Then he's mine. Aunt Carole will be worrying where we are, anyway. You can tell her we ran out to pick-up some food for dinner. I'll make the Major's excuses when I get back with some pizza." With that, Britt turned and stomped up the stairs to the deck.

Rick and Bill followed her to where she stood, ramrod straight by the deck doors. "You could have gone in, you know it's not locked." Rick stepped up to open the door for her. Britt threw him a look of utter disdain before she moved into the cool interior of his cottage.

Britt stood facing the two men, arms folded over her chest, fury darkening her eyes to midnight blue.

Rick gestured for her to sit down but she shook her head "no." He pulled up a chair at the table. Bill sat on the couch, his eyes full of questions for Rick and concern for Britt. He patted the cushion next to him. "Honey, why don't you sit here next to me? Rick can get us something cold to drink."

"Thank you, but no." Her reply to her uncle was cool but civil. "I don't want to sit, and I don't want anything to drink." She turned to Rick. "I do want to know what makes you think you have the right to go digging around in my life and my career."

"I don't have the right. But, I do have the need to find out who hurt you and why he's still walking around alive." Restrained anger was evident in Rick's voice. Britt shrank back from the cold vengeance in his eyes. But there was steel in her voice.

"The man who *hurt* me is dead. He was killed in the blast resulting from the device he threw in the room where Nadia and I were with the women. Or he died from the shots fired by my unit when they arrived moments later. End of story."

"No," Rick said, rising. He reached out to take her elbow, to put her next to her uncle for what he was sure would be a devastating revelation. She jerked her arm out of his grasp.

"Brittany!" Bill's deep voice was sharp and clear. "I know you are pissed off at Rick and probably at me, too. And you're probably justified in most, if not all, of that anger. But stop your temper tantrum right now and come sit here next to me so we can hear what he has to tell us. You can bite his head off later if you want."

Her glance flew between the two men, noting the regret in Bill's eyes and the resolve on Rick's face. She moved stiffly to the sofa and sat down, back ramrod straight. "Okay," she looked over at Rick as he sat down in the chair across from the sofa, "what do you think you know about that night?"

He looked as uncomfortable and full of regret as any man she had ever spoken with. No, he looked like the doctor in Germany who told her, finally, that Nadia was dead. "Shit," she thought, just as he began to speak, "he knows."

"Yes, the insurgent who tossed the grenade into the room is dead. He died from the blast. Your unit didn't shoot him or anyone in that room. They didn't arrive until several minutes after your first call and almost two minutes after your second call. The officer in charge of the mission, Lieutenant Colonel Jonathan Gable, dismissed your first call as 'female hysteria' and did not respond until your second call. And he did so reluctantly. Later, he initially reported that there had been no calls for assistance from you or Nadia. But, fortunately, the radioman was questioned again, and he confirmed your story. And reported what Gable had said about your first request for back-up. By then, you were in Walter Reed, soon to be discharged. They removed Gable from command and shipped him back to the States. His career ascent is over. He's a desk jockey at DOD." Rick was staring at her, as if he was waiting for her to burst into tears or throw something through a window. Or leap across the distance between them and rip his throat out.

Britt sat frozen. The two men were waiting for a response from her. She had nothing to say, no words to tell them that she already knew most of Rick's story. Then she smiled, because of the information that her radioman had spoken up and had confirmed her version of the events; he had stood with her.

"You knew." Rick almost spat the words. "You knew it was Gable. And you did nothing. Why?" Sickened realization spread over his face. "My God, were you covering for him?"

"Fuck you!" She spat the words in his face. Britt didn't realize she was rising until she felt her uncle's hand on her arm, pulling her back down next to him. He continued to grip her arm, as tremors of anger rippled through her. "I wasn't protecting him. I hope he rots in hell, after a slow and painful death, disgraced and alone. I was protecting the women."

"What women, honey?" The question was Bill's. "Who did you think you needed to protect?"

"The sergeant who told me what was in the final incident report. It was confidential information, but she let me know the truth when she notified me that Alex was being sent over here from Kandahar. All I had been told, officially, was that further investigation supported my statements that I called for assistance. Back-up was sent to my location but arrived too late to stop the breach and take out the enemy. If I filed a complaint that Jake had ignored my calls for assistance, I'd be asked how I knew that he had ignored them. I'd be asked why he would ignore such a request from one of his soldiers, why I was questioning his motives. I'd have to say I knew about his hysterical female remark—and let me say for that alone I want to cut off his balls and shove them down his throat—and I'd have to reveal the source of my information. She's a staff sergeant, career Army, supporting two kids Stateside. She was one of Jake's targets, too, and she came forward when I filed my complaint to save Alex. They could have destroyed her for telling me. Even if I didn't say how I knew, they'd trace it to her pretty fast and then she'd be in a shit load of trouble." Britt dropped her face in her hands, overwhelmed by the courage and loyalty the other woman had showed in giving Britt confidential information.

Then her head jerked up. She glared at Rick. "How did you find out? Did you go through her? She'll be busted in rank, probably dishonorably discharged...."

Rick interrupted her. "I didn't use her. I saw her name in the files I accessed; she signed the complaint against Gable that you and the lieutenant filed. I figured she knew what had happened during the investigation since a lot of the paperwork went through her office. And I saw what she did to expedite Alex's release to you and his transport Stateside. I wasn't going to let any of this fallout touch her. I went through other channels and I'm not telling you who or where. I have people to protect, too."

Bill spoke up, interrupting what was surely to be another verbal attack by Britt. "Rick, you found out what this prick Gable did and didn't do and I'll go on record that I want first dibs on cutting his balls off, if he even has any, but what is his status now? Is anything going to be done to him?"

"Well, here's the beauty of all this, though there's little in this tale that has any beauty, except that Britt didn't get killed. Seems that fucker Gable has been riding a desk at DOD for a while, ingratiating himself to his superiors, which he excels at doing. He'd probably finish his career in administration, but the Army is starting this new program. The Security Force Assistance Brigade. A permanent unit solely dedicated to advising and assisting partner nations in developing their security force capability from the tactical to ministerial level. Lieutenant Colonel Gable decided to apply for a command position in the SFAB. That's what made it easier for me to track him down and *access* his files; they were under review based on his application. I just made sure that the radioman's statement was, shall I say, a highlighted portion of his records and, trust me, they had it buried pretty deep."

Rick rose and came over to sit next to Britt. "Pretty soon, maybe even by now, people in command positions who will not overlook Gable's actions that night or his cover-up attempts thereafter, will be calling him in and reopening the investigation. You won't be involved since the record shows you followed proper procedure and the radioman is backing up your story, as far as it goes. You were injured when back-up finally arrived so there's nothing you can add. The sergeant has no role in this new investigation at all. And it seems this is not the first questionable incident that involved Gable. He's done in the Army, at the very least. And he may be looking at some time behind bars." Rick's hand rested lightly on Britt's leg. "Is that enough for you? It won't bring Nadia back and it won't give you a good leg and shoulder, but the fucker will pay for what he did. If you want more...." Rick's voice trailed off, but the implication was clear. If Britt wanted physical harm to befall Gable, he would see that it happened. Likely with his own two hands.

"No. I had made my peace with him being stuck behind a desk, no more promotions, no glory. It was enough because it protected other women who had come forward against him on my behalf. This is better, especially if you can find a way to let the sergeant know."

"I can, and I will." Rick patted her leg and rose again, stepping around her to face Bill. "Is that enough for you, sir?"

"It is not. I would like to see him dead. But, it's not my decision and I can live with this if Brittany can. Although, if I ever run into the prick, he won't be getting up." Bill leaned over and hugged his niece. "I wish you hadn't felt the need to carry this one alone, honey. I understand but I want you to know that your aunt and I are ready to do anything for you. We love you."

Tears glistened in Britt's eyes as she hugged her uncle back. "I love you, too."

"Well, I'd best get next door and tell Carole its pizza for dinner. And I think I'll take Alex for a stroll down the beach. I need some fresh air." Bill shook Rick's hand before he left the living room and ambled across the deck and down to the beach.

Britt stood, too. "Well, I'm going to walk down to the pizza place and get some dinner for my aunt and uncle." She smiled sadly at him. "I thought you and I might have a chance, Marine. I was almost in love with you." She held up a hand when Rick started to speak. "As you've learned, I've had to deal with betrayal. By a man and then by the institution I loved and respected. I've just learned to trust again, thanks to Kit and Alex, and I was beginning to trust you. But, you destroyed that by going behind my back, investigating my past and jeopardizing people I care about. If I can't trust you, I can't love you. If I can't love you, I can't spend any more time with you." She turned to the doors, stopping to gaze out at the beach. Without turning, she said, "You stay to this end of the beach and I'll stay to my side. We ought to be able to co-exist at least for the rest of the summer."

Before she could step through the door, Rick's voice stopped her. "That's it? That's how you end this? Because you can't trust me? You knew I would see through that half-ass story you told me about Kandahar and the attack. You had to know, given who and what I am, that I would discover the truth. And that I would do something about it. It's what I do. I protect."

"No," she turned on him. "You control. You think it's all about protection but it's about control. That way you don't have to feel too much—you don't have to feel anything. The people in your life are just objectives for you to overcome, neutralize, and leave. Another mission."

"How can you say that to me? You know what I felt...feel...for you. The control I've given up, let you take, to be with you. I trusted you enough to do that. But you haven't trusted me, Britt."

She stared at him. "What do you mean? I let you into my house, my body. I even trusted you with Alex."

"Flight 93, Britt." She felt all the blood drain out of her face. "Why didn't you tell me about your parents? I found out from your uncle, just today. When were you going to trust me enough to tell me about that?"

Leaning back against the door to hold herself up, Britt just stared at him. "You're right. It's too painful for me to talk about, to re-live. I see them every day in my mind, laughing like newlyweds, climbing into Bill and Carole's car on the street outside my apartment in Manhattan. Off on their great adventure. To San Francisco. Then I see the burned scar in a field in Pennsylvania. All that was left of them. And I feel anger and hate and hopelessness. Every day for years. I've been able to put that behind me since Saratoga. But, I guess not enough to let you in, Marine."

Britt shook her head sadly. "I guess that's us, Rick. Two wounded warriors, with hearts that are too scarred to feel enough anymore to trust. To love." She threw him a weary salute and walked out the door.

CHAPTER TWENTY-FOUR

July dragged by, the days fading into each other. Britt complained to Alex about the dog days of summer. He did nothing but pant in the shade of the deck. But at night, they curled up together on her big bed, neither able to admit that they missed the Marine.

The morning after their confrontation, Rick's dusty Jeep had still been parked in his driveway. Uncle Bill and Aunt Carole insisted on taking her out for a big breakfast and she didn't have the heart to tell them she had no appetite. Early in the afternoon, they left to continue their journey to Boston. Out on the deck, waiting for her aunt to fuss with one more thing in the cottage, her uncle pulled her aside.

"How are you today, honey? Did you and Rick have words after I left? Don't be too hard on him. I think he did what he did out of genuine feelings for you."

"I'm sure he had the best intentions, Uncle Bill. I think we just need a little time to think all this through. Don't worry about me. I've still got Alex." She reached down to pet the dog who was wedged between them. "And you and Aunt Carole."

"Yes, honey, you do. And your cousins, Bill and Andrew. They're no more than an hour away from here. You call them if you need anything. And your aunt and I will be coming back through the first of August. She wants to drive up to Maine after the wedding. She's got it in her head to see Kennebunkport and Campobello Island. I think she's stalking ex-presidents or something. She's been watching too much PBS."

Britt laughed at her aunt's new presidential obsession. It was the last time she laughed. The next morning when she went around the front of the house to put the garbage out, Rick's Jeep was gone. That afternoon, the cleaning crew swept through his cottage, leaving with two black bags of trash. After that, his lovely beach cottage was empty. The light over the doors on the deck came on every night at dusk and were off as soon as dawn's first rays crept over the horizon.

"It's just as well," she told Alex every morning when the dog looked across the deck to the house that had become a second home to him. "It would have only been a matter of time before Rick was off on some other adventure, some other mission to save the world. He can't save himself, so he'll try to control everyone else. Damn stubborn Marine." Still, she found herself sitting on her deck every evening, facing his cottage, waiting for the light to come on, hoping it would signal more than the arrival of evening.

One night, almost two weeks after Rick's abrupt departure, Britt saw a man coming out of the cottage next door. He paused to lock the door. As he was crossing the deck, he looked over and saw Britt. Smiling, he sent her a brisk salute. She recognized him as the man she had seen a time or two around the cottage before Rick had arrived. She nodded and smiled at him from her seat on the chaise lounge.

Alex was by her side, snoozing on the still warm deck, but as the man descended the stairs from Rick's house, he poked his head up. Within moments he was bounding down the stairs and heading across the sand. Britt called out to him, but it was obvious that her dog thought Rick had returned. She was moving across the deck when she saw Alex come to a skidding stop in front of the man. The two stared at each other until the man looked up at her and called out "Hey, I know Alex. Rick introduced us one day. I'm Mick and I'm a lot nicer than Rick."

"Alex, it's okay. This is Mick. He's a friend, remember? It's okay."
Britt called down to the dog, who eyed the man for another moment
then turned back to his own stairs, his posture far less exuberant.
Mick followed a few paces behind 'til he was at the base of the steps.
"Rick told me a little about you. May I come up for a few minutes?"
When Britt nodded her assent, the big man slowly climbed the steps
behind Alex.

"Damn stairs. I still get a little short of breath after all these years."
He aimed his charming smile at Britt. "I lost part of a lung in Iraq.
And," he held up his right hand, "part of a finger. Small price to pay. At
least I didn't get dead."

She motioned him to sit down on a chaise lounge. "Can I get you
something to drink?"

"If you have anything cold, I wouldn't say no." It was a hot, humid
beach night. The ocean breeze was barely stirring the air. Britt
returned from the kitchen with two glasses of icy lemonade.

"Thank you, ma'am. That will do the trick," Mick said, reaching for
the glass. He drained half of it in one gulp.

"How do you know Rick?' Britt was eyeing him with interest.

"We met in the Marines, right out of college. I was an engineer,
into tanks and armored vehicles. Anything that moved and fired
weapons and I was happy." He took another sip of his drink. "Rick
sometimes caught a ride with me and my guys but mostly he liked
skulking about, talking gibberish to the natives, sneaking in and out
of enemy territory. Then he'd let me know where to point my artillery
and we'd send the bastards straight to Hell."

She smiled. "That sounds like Rick. Telling people what to do,
taking control of the situation."

Mick stared at her for a moment. "You know with me and my
guys, we were surrounded by armor. We had guns and tanks and
ammo, and we could crush or blast anything that got in our way. We
went out on a mission, we knew there was a chance that some of us
wouldn't come back, there's always that possibility in war. But, Rick
and his guys? They went out to face the enemy sometimes with
nothing but their wits and their wile. Never knowing for sure who

was an ally and who was going to slit your throat, not knowing where you were headed or how long it would be before you were back speaking English and eating pizza in a mess tent. And not knowing if your next target was going to be hardened men who had been fighting for years or boy soldiers not even in their teens."

She didn't know what to say. Mick sat there looking out at the ocean in the fading light. When he finally spoke again, his voice was soft. "He's the best man I ever knew, the best soldier, the most loyal patriot, the most caring friend. And he's got demons I wouldn't have the courage to face. I never saw him smile as much as he was smiling while he was here this month. Maybe you could cut him a little slack."

Mick wiped his mouth with the back of his hand and stood. "Anyway, thank you for the lemonade. It hit the spot. Better than those fruit smoothies my daughters are always making me drink. I know there's kale or some green shit hidden in them." He bent over to pet Alex's big head. At the top of the stairs, he turned and smiled at Britt. "Rick's up in Cambridge, checking his place out and visiting with his cousins. Nice women. He'll be back the first of August. In case you're interested. Good night, Captain." He saluted smartly and disappeared into the night.

CHAPTER TWENTY-FIVE

For the second time in less than thirty days, Rick was driving onto Long Beach Island in his dusty Jeep, just as the sun was setting behind him. Springsteen was singing plaintively about the river and wondering if a dream was a lie if it don't come true. "Hell, yeah," Rick muttered.

But, once again, as always, when he caught the scent of the Atlantic, when he heard the waves crashing on the shore, a kind of peace settled over him. Come what may, he always had this place, this refuge. Pulling into his drive, he put the Jeep in park and rested his head on his hands on the wheel. He didn't know what he'd find when he went up the stairs and looked from his deck to the cottage next door. With the ease of someone who traveled light, he grabbed his worn duffel from the seat behind him and headed up to meet his fate. He heard the barking before he stepped onto his deck.

Rick dropped his duffel at the top of the stairs and went to the edge of his deck. Alex was prancing in the sand at the foot of Britt's staircase, barking like crazy. Rick saw a bright lime green tennis ball fly through the open door of her beach house. The big yellow dog took off across the beach, chasing it like a dream. Rick moved into the circle of light cast by the fixture above his deck doors. Glancing over at the house where so much had changed in his life made his heart constrict. Where was she?

As if she had heard his silent question, Britt emerged from the open doors clad in the same loose, brightly printed caftan she'd been wearing that first night. The ocean breeze pressed the flowing fabric against her long, lean body, caressing her full breasts. Her silvery hair was piled atop her head like a crown, but the wind had torn several strands loose and they floated veil-like around her face. She lifted a hand to push the hair out of her face and that is when she saw him.

He was scruffy and dusty from the trip, he hadn't shaved in days. A gray T-shirt, softened from a hundred washes, clung to his broad chest. His jeans were older than the shirt, almost worn through at the knees, and the ancient boat shoes he wore were soft as glove leather. He felt like he looked: an aging warrior finally coming home, looking for shelter, his last enemy vanquished, the trappings of war left behind.

They stood staring at each other. He didn't know whether he should wave or salute, blow a kiss or just call out "hello." She hadn't moved, her hand was still held against her forehead, keeping the hair from her eyes, as if she couldn't bear for anything to impede her view of him.

Alex's delighted yips broke the silence between them. He was trotting across the beach to Britt's cottage, when he stopped suddenly, staring at Rick's place. Then, he was off in a frenzied rush to take the steps two at a time. He jumped up on his back legs, his paws planted firmly on Rick's chest, his long tongue lapping at Rick's neck.

Rick grabbed the dog's big head, rubbing his ears, crooning nonsense sounds to him. It was so good to see that Alex had not forgotten him, had not turned against him for leaving so abruptly. "If only your mama feels the same way, boy. I might have a chance."

Satisfied that his friend had returned, Alex dropped back down on all fours. He ran over to the edge of the deck as if checking that Britt knew Rick was back. His back and forth continued for a few moments, then as if to signal the humans that it was their turn to greet each other, he came up to Rick. The dog nudged Rick's hand with his head and then clambered down the steps. He paused at the bottom of the stairs, as if to ask why Rick wasn't following him, then ran home to Britt.

The dog galvanized them both into action. Rick crossed the deck, moved down the stairs and across the sand between the two houses. He stopped at the foot of Britt's stairs, looking up into her piquant face. Not knowing what to say, an inane remark escaped his lips. "Hot enough for you?"

Her eyebrows raised in amused surprise. She stared at him for a long moment, then burst into laughter. Shaking her head in disbelief, she said, "You leave without notice, you're away for weeks, you come back without any warning and all you've got is weather?" Turning away from him, she threw an invitation over her shoulder, "I need a drink, if you want one, you better come up here out of the heat." With that, she disappeared inside.

Rick was up the stairs in a second and appeared in the open door of the living room just as she was removing a bottle of white wine from the fridge. He closed the door behind him and moved into the room. As Britt reached for two wine glasses from the rack, it seemed to him that there was a slight tremor in her hands. *Good.* He wanted her to be affected by him, he wanted to breach the last of her defenses. She handed him a glass of bubbly Vinho Verde then settled herself on the overstuffed sofa, one leg tucked under her.

"So, Marine, what brings you back to the Shore in the midst of a heat wave?" She took a sip of wine. Her hands were still unsteady.

Rick sat at the other end of the sofa. Alex looked at the space between them and, as if ascertaining that there was not enough room for him, sauntered over to the bedroom door and disappeared. "You, Britt. You brought me back."

"If that was true, you wouldn't have left." Accusatory words, but uttered with a soft smile

"You were the one who walked away from me, darlin'. I don't think anything has ever wounded me as much as the sight of you turning your back on me." His voice cracked with emotion.

"Your friend, Mick, came by. He seems like a nice guy, Alex liked him. He told me you were in New York, in Cambridge."

He was taken aback that she knew where he had been, but she didn't seem to be making the connection. Couldn't she see the change in him? "Yes, I needed to check on the property and I hadn't seen my cousins in several months. Tourists have discovered Cambridge and the antiques shop is doing a record business. Nellie, my grandmother, would be so proud. My cousins, Maggie and Colleen, think we should expand the merchandise up to the second floor, maybe make it an antique clothes boutique. Seems there's quite a market for antique clothes these days."

"Where would you live? Here at the Shore all year?" She looked at him as if the possibility was of some interest to her.

"I looked at some property in Saratoga while I was up there. For the last few years, I've been thinking about turning the whole building in Cambridge over to my cousins. I'd like a little more space and the girls have worked so hard in the antiques shop, I figured I'd just give them my share of the building."

"I don't understand. You left here because of me or you left here to take care of family business in New York?" Britt was shaking her head.

"I left here because I needed to think about what you had said. And I needed to find the answers to some questions I've had for many years. Questions about control." She didn't look as surprised as he thought she would.

"Mick said you felt the need to control everything because so many of the battles you fought were non-traditional, like guerrilla warfare and clandestine operations where you don't know who the enemy is or where you'll find him. The only certainty you had was you and your abilities. Not like Mick with his tanks."

Rick smiled. "Mick loved those damn tanks. Show him a target and he could blast it from any distance." His smile faded. "It's different when it's hand-to-hand, when you look your enemy in his eye."

"And your enemy turns out to be a kid or a woman." Britt wasn't smiling, either. "And your men, your team, can't deal with that. It's a no-win situation. So, you take it all on yourself."

"This wasn't what I planned to talk to you about when I came back here. Then I saw you on the deck and you were so beautiful and I wanted you so much, I couldn't remember anything I wanted to tell you. I just wanted to hold you."

"I saw you, in the light on your deck and I wasn't sure it was you. I've watched for you every night since you left, and I thought I'd dreamed you there because I've missed you so much." She put up her hand when he reached for her. "I've never stopped wanting you, Rick, that was never our problem. Well, at least it wasn't once we talked out the control issues. But, I can't just have sex with you. There has to be more."

"There is more. It was never just sex, not with you. I felt something for you from the first moment I saw you."

"We've been over this," she said softly. "If I can't trust you, I can't love you. If I can't love you, I can't be with you."

"You can trust me. You can trust me now, Britt. Because *I* trust me. I'm not afraid anymore that everyone around me is in danger and needs to be protected. I know I can't control everything. I've made my peace with that."

Disbelief and hope were written across her face. He took her hand and this time she didn't pull away.

"While I was driving around Saratoga, looking at property, I remembered what you had told me. I made a few calls. Then I decided to drop in on some old friends of yours. I stopped by Saratoga War Horse." Britt's mouth opened then closed without a word and her eyes filled with tears. "Kit says hello and he misses you, but he likes me better."

"What? You did the program? They matched you with Kit? I don't believe it."

"I didn't believe it, either. I listened to you tell me about the program and what a transformation it meant for you and I thought it was a nice little fairy tale, but that it wouldn't work for someone who had seen what I'd seen and done what I'd done. But, after you walked away from me, I knew I needed a miracle. I thought I might find it where I grew up but there was no one there who I could talk to about my experiences, my doubts, and my fears. No one I trusted. So, I looked the place up. They found a spot for me and I was in."

Britt's face was glowing like a kid on Christmas morning. She raised their joined hands to her lips and kissed his, her tears splashing against his fingers.

"You were right. What happened can't really be explained. It was like a switch inside me was turned back on. I feel like I got my equilibrium back, I'm on even ground. I'm not fighting shadows anymore. I can tell you now what I knew when you walked away from me but that I was too afraid to admit. I love you. I love you, Britt."

"I love *you*, Rick. God, I love you so much. Welcome home," She slid across the couch and into his arms.

For the first time in many years, Rick felt no urge to restrain or control. All he wanted was to hold her and kiss her. His mouth found hers. She sighed and opened her lips to welcome his questing tongue. The kiss deepened, Britt's hands were in his hair, trying to hold on as he ravaged her mouth. Breaking away, trailing his lips over her face and down her neck, across her collarbone, he finally reached the V-neck of her loose robe. Pulling it to the side, he found her breast. His lips and teeth fastened on her nipple and he sucked and nipped until she was moaning his name.

"Shhh," he laughingly whispered, "you'll wake the dog!"

"Fuck the dog," was her passionate response when his hands started to slide up her thighs.

"No, darlin', but I'll be happy to fuck you." And his fingers plunged into her silky heat. Within moments her moans were muffled screams and she came hard against his hand. Rick pushed her down onto the sofa and rose up to unfasten his jeans and yank them off. They fell with a soft thud on the floor and then Rick was kissing his way up her thighs. His tongue flicked once against her throbbing center and her long, low utterance of his name was all the encouragement that he needed. Rising up, he slid into her. Britt arched her back and wrapped her legs around his waist. His cock was buried deep in her throbbing heat. Rick looked down into the flushed face of his lover, her eyes bright with passion, her lips swollen from his kisses.

"I love you, Captain." He moved in her, all the way into her.

"I love you, too, Major. Now, shut up and kiss me." Britt's lips covered his face with tiny kisses.

"Who's the one taking control now?" Rick's taunting words were drowned out when her mouth fastened on his. Her tongue thrust in and out of his mouth as his cock thrust in and out of her slick passage. When he was about to explode, Britt clenched her muscles around him and milked every drop from him, her hips pistoning against him as her own orgasm swept through her. Rick collapsed on top of her, rolling her to the side so his full weight did not rest on her.

They lay in each other's arms as their breathing calmed. Rick reached over and fumbled in his jeans. Britt giggled. "What are you looking for, a condom? It's a little late for that, don't you think?" Shaking his head, Rick straightened back up and took her hand. He slid an antique opal surrounded by sapphires onto her ring finger. "I was worried that it might be too late for this. I found it in the shop, it's from an estate sale. I don't know how old it is, but it reminded me of your eyes."

Her eyes were wide with stunned joy. "I love it. It's perfect."

"We never talked about the future, but this ring is my promise to you of a future together. Whatever and wherever you want your future to be, I want to share it with you. Promise me you'll let me." He bent to kiss her hand, where the ring sparkled in the moonlight streaming in through the wide glass doors.

Britt took his face in both her hands and kissed him. "I promise that you and I will build a future together based on love and trust."

Rick wrapped her in his arms, her head snuggled against his shoulder, her long legs entwined with his, and marveled at the miracle of their love. Two wounded warriors, veterans of countless battles, surrendering their hearts to each other, finally at peace.

THE END

ALSO BY MORGAN MALONE

Cocktales: An After 50 Dating Memoir

Out of Control: Kat's Story

Unanswered Prayers

Shoulder to Lean On: A Barefoot Bay Novella

Need You Now: A Barefoot Bay Novella

Color My World: A Barefoot Bay Novella

ABOUT THE AUTHOR

Morgan Malone has been reading romance since the age of twelve when she snuck her mother's copy of Gone with the Wind under the bed covers to read by flashlight. A published author at the age of eight, Morgan waited fifty years, including thirty as an administrative law judge and counsel, to write her next work of fiction. Retired from her legal career with a small NYS agency, Morgan lives near Saratoga Springs, NY, with her faithful Labrador retriever, Marley. When not writing "seasoned romance" about men and women over 35 who are finding love for the last, and maybe the first, time in their lives, Morgan is penning her memoirs, painting watercolors, or hanging out with her delightful grandson.

Visit Morgan online:
morganmaloneauthor.com
www.facebook.com/MorganMaloneAuthor
www.Twitter.com/MMaloneAuthor

Made in the USA
Coppell, TX
06 May 2021